I0670957

Zombie Survival Crew:

Undead Is Not An Option

Edited by
Juliette Terzieff &
LK Gardner-Griffie

This anthology is dedicated to all of the fans of @TheZSC for coming along on this fantastic ride as we explore the twisted, dark world of the undead. We couldn't do it without you!

ISBN: 978-0-9842383-6-1
Zombie Survival Crew Anthology
Undead Is Not An Option
Copyright © 2011 by Zombie Survival Crew ™
Shanlian WordLit Press

Cover art by Samantha Lahue
Photos by Anthony Guajardo on pages 8, 60, 68, 95, and 120
Photos by Anthony Guajardo with modifications by LK Gardner-Griffie on pages 25, 56, and 92
Art work by Samantha Lahue on page 21
Art work by Sonya May on page 42
Art work by Natalie Cutrufello on pages 50, 75, and 112

Table of Contents

Foreword

IronE Singleton & Juliette Terzieff

We are our own worst enemy. For no logical reason we—our collective human family—continue down a long and winding road toward annihilation. Better weapons. Less trust. More fear. Panic. Selfishness. Lack of preparation. Ignorance. All of these belong buried in a landfill, but sadly remain firmly secured in our collective arsenal.

And now as wars unfold in every corner of the world, each addition to the body count increases the fear, and advances notions of the end of the world. It convinces us—even if we are too afraid to admit it in public—that we will be the source of our ultimate earthly destruction.

The fear is hardly new. In fact, it has been taking solid form for decades. Creeping like a ghoul from the grave with every advance in defense technology, with every master of hate to climb the pulpit. And now the walking dead have exploded around us—eclipsing the resurgence of romantic monsters of the past couple decades. Lestat, Edward, and their vampire brethren prowl around the edges, but the shambling hordes control the streets. They are us, and we are them. We cannot escape the truths they reveal.

****

In the aftermath of World War II and throughout the Cold War years, writers and filmmakers crafted some of the most disturbing post-apocalyptic scenarios ever put to paper or film. The social commentary stung, but rang true. Was there anything beyond the bounds of human cruelty? Given the evidence of places like Dachau and Hiroshima, really, what limits could possibly remain? Through art these visionaries asked people to see beyond the face-level horror to the real monsters in their stories.

Take British author John Wyndham's book *The Chrysalids* (1955) set in an über-conservative post-nuclear society where any hint of physical or mental abnormality is considered blasphemy. Those unfortunate enough to display any genetic variance are forced to undergo sterilization, banishment or are killed outright. Family members turn each other in out of fear. Fathers battle sons. Mothers are forced to give up their children. Out of the question? Hardly.

Or the stunning black-and-white *Last Man on Earth* (1964) based on Richard Matheson's *I Am Legend* in which an increasingly disturbed Vincent Price battles loneliness and sorrow in a Quixotic quest to maintain sanity in a world overrun by vampiric former humans infected by a plague. Desperate to protect his humanity though there is apparently none left in the world. Searching for a reason, a cure, some way to regain a measure of his former life—with no real hope that any sort of happy ending can be possible. Just driven to keep going.

Again is this scenario so far-fetched? No. Not nearly far enough.

And then *he* made his masterpiece. With a modest budget, independent filmmaker George Romero changed the way we would view our world forever with his homage to the political idiocies of the time called *Night of the Living Dead* (1968). With a level of gore previously unseen on the silver screen, Romero changed the zombie genre forever—taking Voodoo rituals out of the fringe and launching an examination of the human spirit that continues to this day. Romero's ghouls obey no master, no priest or priestess. Lurching ever onward. Bloodied hands reach for the next meal. Only the willfully blind could ignore the truths revealed beneath the intestinal gore.

The reanimated dead have no pretensions, no ulterior motives. They are driven by base need. Absent is the politics of their former human lives. Gone are the wants and desires that cause perversion toward other human beings.

****

But what of the walkers that surround us every day? Do you see them? They are not the walkers of the virus-driven Zombiepocalypse. Yet they are all around us. Lurching. Stumbling. Hungry hordes of lost souls. Do you know who they are, how to fight them? How to survive?

It's no easy task in a world gone insane. There are few who know this better than a five-time war correspondent veteran or an inner-city survivor who happened to grow up to battle television zombies as part of his day job. It's a constant fight and my battle-tested writing partner, IronE, isn't afraid to share the lessons he's learned on his journey so far . . .

Breaking News! A customer at a gas station was shot in the chest at point blank range in an attempted robbery. True story. This stuff is as dramatic as a popular television show of mine, *The Walking Dead*, where I play T-Dog (a survivor in a world of zombies). Chaos and mayhem tend to dominate the theme of the show/news . . . multiple gunshots, rape, murder, starvation, car chases, unbelievable explosions, you name it. The only difference is that it is sad and anti-climactic because it is real.

And it could have been me.

I was raised in a destructive environment without a father and dealing with an alcohol and drug-addicted mother in the inner city of Atlanta, GA. I found myself fighting, carrying a pistol and selling drugs with the potential of becoming just as lost and destitute as the individuals contributing to the destruction and insanity flashing before me this very moment on the headline news in 2011. Similar to zombies scavenging the streets on the prowl for their next "fix", many human beings are like lost souls searching for fulfillment. Something, anything, to fill the negative void often created as a result of circumstance; never truly satisfying that hunger/craving for what we know as salvation or enlightenment. It is a distorted reality that depresses our spirits and suppresses the will and true desire of our conscience; unwavering truth and unconditional love.

I remember selling crack to men, women—yes, even pregnant women, and kids . . .although I never gave crack to my mother, unlike my brother, who's been in and out of jail since the age of 14. It was so easy to fall into that "life." It was a kind conditioning similar to a robot doing exactly what it is programmed to do . . . or like a zombie, where impulse and emotion supersede rationality. I knew that life all too well.

The addicts would approach with blank distant eyes with one desire only; crack. And they were willing to do whatever it took to get that crack; steal, kill, etc. The robbers and bangers would watch and prey on the weak for whatever they could get while working folk and the elderly would lock themselves away at home and pray for a better tomorrow. It was either survive or die. I survived. A lot of my friends and family died, including my mom, who died of A.I.D.S. contracted through drug use. She tried to pass the blame of contracting H.I.V. by telling me she'd been raped. She probably was, but I doubt it was the cause. In the 70's and 80's she shot drugs with several of her friends who, eventually, died of it as well. It seemed like the other vices of my neighborhood were extensions of the pervasive drug problem. I understand why. Using drugs was a temporary fix to an otherwise unbearable and miserable existence of destitute poverty. It soothed the pain. Selling drugs was a way to make big, quick money when a minimum wage job just wouldn't do. It was for most, "a way out."

Fortunately, God spared me a horrific demise and I made it out of the inner city and into the University of Georgia, where I gained a greater understanding of this drug phenomenon through extensive knowledge of the Iran Contra Scandal. It was the inner city projects where I became a zombie and then zombie survivor, but in college I realized that this drug epidemic was bigger than the projects. Therefore, this zombie apocalypse was a lot bigger . . . and real.

****

And now here we are. Ripples of protest, deafening calls for change, sweep across the Arab world. Military juntas and repressive leadership in countries including Burma, North Korea and Sudan continue to commit horrific abuses against their people. Soldiers and civilians continue to die every hour of every day in places like Afghanistan and Iraq. Food is scarce. Weather is wacky. Our potable water supply is dwindling.

The world is changing—rapidly—in ways that strike the heart of even the bravest individual. Yet even with the terrifying array of challenges we face there is so much "business as usual."

Politicians trade meaningless banter. In opposition to their political foe(s) and/or counterpart(s), these politicians acknowledge that we are at war, that we are being ravaged by earthquakes, tsunamis, hurricanes, that just like cancer and H.I.V/A.I.D.S, poverty and famine are, too, epidemics that have caused and are causing the deaths of millions of people all over the world. These same politicians laugh during these acknowledgements as if this monumental loss of life is a joke . . . As if their discourse is less about trying to seek a remedy to stop this maddening human destruction and more about political posturing; An attempt to win votes in their next campaign for office all for one reason; **money**. The adage, "attitude reflects leadership" would most appropriately apply in this situation. To whom much is given, much is expected. Our leaders have to be held accountable in a big way for these "zombie-like" mindsets that are being shaped and molded in our world through media-disseminated facts/opinions/propaganda/lies. We, as individuals, are mere reflections of those that lead us. At the same time, only an individual is ultimately responsible for his/her actions, and that is both right and wrong.

Right and wrong? That's an oxymoron. How can that be? It's right because an individual should suffer the consequences for his/her actions. It's wrong because the people we expect to legislate and serve as role models are making unethical and immoral decisions that directly and indirectly affect our individual decisions. Example: An upstanding, hardworking citizen of 20 years chooses to rob a bank in order to pay for his child's heart transplant because he can't afford it, and the medical insurance payment that has been collected from him over that time period does not cover transplants. Or corporations given a bailout by, us, the taxpayers for financial disasters they caused. And for their reckless behavior, these corporations' executives get pay raises, big bonus checks and severance packages and, we, the taxpayers get . . . layoffs, depleted 401k funds, ruined pensions, foreclosures, etc.

Ultimately, it all boils down to choices. Either we can allow the madness and chaos in our society continue to control us like zombies, or rise above it and do all we can to counter and rectify it as zombie survivors. Perhaps it is only natural in an era of such tumult that demands profound decisions from each and every one of us that our greatest fears—death, decay, loss of control—reemerge as central themes in contemporary art like you'll find in this work. We are dealing with uncomfortable subjects, difficult questions. Do we choose to band together and prepare to meet the challenges? We hope this book will help you choose.

Our family and loved ones motivate and inspire us every step of the way. For IronE—a beautiful, intelligent and devoted wife, Commaleta, and three children (Heavven, Nevvaeh, Ethereal); for Juliette—friends and mentors Sherry and Drita, and the memory of beloved parents, George and Vaerie, and son, Haris. They have convinced us that being a zombie survivor is the only choice. United we stand and divided we fall.

PEACE & LOVE!
IronE Singleton& Juliette Terzieff
ZSC Commanders, Green & Red Brigades

ZOMBIE SURVIVAL CREW™ CLASSIFIED WARNING ORDER

Compiled by Special Operative Kelene Toups

Summary:

The Military Warning Order is a preliminary notice of an action that is to follow. Warning orders help subordinate units and their staff prepare for new missions. Warning orders maximize planning time, provide essential details of the impending operation, and detail major time-line events that accompany mission execution. Warning Orders are sent to military units to inform them of their upcoming tasks and duties particularly in battle or for reconnaissance.

Based on information received while monitoring the Zombie Survival Crew™ website, this department of a secret government agency (which at this time will remain unnamed) has chosen the Zombie Survival Crew™ to lead the first official assault on the undead enemy. Your task and instructions are delineated in the orders, and should be followed precisely to discontinue the proliferation of the enemy.

About the author:

Kelene Toups has been in the Navy for fourteen years, and has spent over half that time with the Seabees, who use military warning orders to ready the battalions for wartime operations. While not formally trained in creative writing, Kelene thought a warning order would be perfect for the operation the Zombie Survival Crew™ is readying. She lives in San Diego, CA with her husband and three children and can be found on twitter under the handle: @kelenetoups

Weapon of Choice: The AA-12 Automatic shotgun

CLASSIFIED MESSAGE

TASK ORGANIZATION: Zombie Survival Crew (ZSC)

1. SITUATION: Several weeks ago, your organization was called upon to build a force and recruit for the imminent zombie apocalypse. Your orders are to serve as a front line force to protect the living, and annihilate the undead.

    a. <u>Enemy Forces</u>

        (1) Recent reports indicate attacks and sightings in major cities in the United States and other countries around the globe. International recruiting has ensured our allies are well prepared for the attack. And these allies have pledged their full support to the ZSC. Intelligence obtained from our most recent reconnaissance mission suggests a large-scale attack is approaching. The Zombie Survival Crew is now, officially, on full alert. **THIS IS NOT A DRILL.**

(2) The enemy, easily identified by their pale grey skin, unhealed wounds, shuffling gait and colorless eyes, travels in packs and is extremely dangerous. Use maximum caution when approaching large numbers; strive to isolate the enemy or reduce to small groups for ease of dispatch. Our research subject has shown the enemy possesses an excellent sense of smell and hearing, poor vision, nonexistent thought process and an insatiable appetite for human flesh. These vital bits of intelligence will aid you in combat against the enemy; use these weaknesses to your full advantage to neutralize the strength of the enemy and diminish the chance of increase in numbers. The most effective means of destruction is to discontinue the neurotransmission process, accomplished by destruction of the brain. I.e. axe blow, bullet, pick axe, crossbow etc…

(3) Recent intelligence reports indicate enemy forces are increasing faster than originally anticipated, with the potential to reach epidemic proportions. The lethal virus is introduced to the host from the saliva of an infected enemy by means of a bite during an attack.

b. Friendly Forces

(1) A small group of survivors in the Atlanta area, originally thought to be massacred by the enemy, has proven to be highly knowledgeable, and efficient at destroying the enemy. Before the untimely destruction of the Center for Disease Control (CDC), they procured vital information that will be highly valuable to the ZSC's mission. Immediately apprehend and transport captives to ZSC headquarters for intelligence debriefing.

(2) Last seen leaving Atlanta to an undisclosed location, the group may attempt to contact scientists in France based on a real-time transmission intercepted from the CDC prior to the destruction of the center.

(3) Approach the group with caution; they are armed and wary of other survivors. The group is comprised of civilians and may be unaware of the existence of The ZSC. Women and children are also present in this group.

(4) Due to the highly successful recruiting campaign, we have international allies, with Brazil pledging the largest numbers of reinforcements and armaments. Brazil, currently, your closest ally should be called upon without hesitation.

2. MISSION:

(1) To openly engage and eradicate any enemy encountered. The National Armory is at the complete disposal of The ZSC. Arm your command with weapons appropriate for successful execution of this mission to include shotguns, handguns, long range rifles, grenades, claymore mines, machetes, compound bows and of course crossbows. For weapons requiring ammunition, conserve when possible as replenishment routes are slow and may eventually be interrupted.

(2) To plan evacuation and escape routes from major cities to include urban towns along route, and to ensure discipline and order in the event an escape is necessary.

3. EXECUTION:
The ZSC must accomplish this mission by launching day/night patrols to assess the strength of enemy numbers. Immediate contact to ZSC Headquarters is essential to ascertain the phase of the impending apocalypse. Each patrol must be in receipt of the detailed contingency plans for patrol capture or ZSC member infection, prior to breaking camp. Once patrols break camp, they will no longer be under the protection of a large arsenal.

DEPARTMENT OF
UNNAMED SECRET
GOVERNMENT AGENCY

4. ADMINISTRATION:

   a. Wounded in Action (WIAs)

   (1) Non Infected: Every attempt should be made to safely escort personnel who are injured in the line of duty. Designate an area in Headquarters to be utilized as a sick-bay for convalescence of ZSC members. Contact should be made with civilians during patrols to secure locations for hasty designated safety zones during patrols.

   (2) Infected: Personnel who are infected by the enemy, i.e. bite, blood splatter or other means of transmission, should be quarantined until infectious process is completed. Quarantine will be in a heavily protected and impenetrable area, until the infectious process has concluded, and destruction of the enemy can occur.

   b. Killed in Action (KIAs) - Corpses should be burned on-site to prevent spread of infection.

5. COMMAND:

DEPARTMENT OF
UNNAMED SECRET
GOVERNMENT AGENCY

(1) ZSC Commander-in-chief will remain at ZSC headquarters.

(2) Brigade Commanders will patrol with ZSC crew members and will be directly responsible for the crew members listed in their brigades.

ZOMBIE SURVIVAL CREW, THESE ARE YOUR ORDERS. EXPEDITE THESE ORDERS IN THE SAFEST WAY POSSIBLE. THE FUTURE OF HUMANITY DEPENDS ON IT.

The Changing
by Jim Bronyaur

What would you do if you were stuck in a tree house, with a complete stranger who is somewhat annoying but a bona fide optimist, a chest full of rocks, and a horde of zombies waiting below? Louie, the optimist, is certain the government is working on a cure for the zombies or a rescue plan, but Arnie keeps mulling over the question, *what could be worse than zombies? The Changing* by Jim Bronyaur answers the question, but leaves you with this one: will you draw blood gnawing on your knuckle by the time you reach the end?

About the author:

Jim Bronyaur lives in Pennsylvania and sits at a desk in a corner writing lots of horror. He's been published over forty times, all of which could be found at his site www.JimBronyaur.com. Those who dare to speak with him can on twitter @jimbronyaur.

Jim's weapon of choice is old school bad-ass... the machete! :)

Nothing like getting inches from a zombie's stinky, rotting corpse and then slashing it with a machete.

The Changing

After the rocks...

Without order, chaos would ensue. It was human nature, maybe instinct, maybe that extra little bit of work creation put into us, but give a man an inch and he'll probably try to take more. Toss in the idea of the world ending and now you've got a whole new bag of shit to deal with.

Arnie noticed the beginning of the chaos after the second rock Louie threw at a zombie. Calm with the first throw, he pretended to be a baseball pitcher. Arnie didn't like nor understand baseball but with the growing group of zombies below them, he'd take a long, hot day at a ballpark anytime.

Louie's second throw was filled with rage. He barely took aim and cursed so much and so fast, the words mixed together. By the time he threw the rock, his body sweated and shook. The rock pegged a zombie in the shoulder and the thing fell over but climbed right back up.

"Three," Arnie said. "Hey, we should consider the rules again. Is it just three? Or should you get three for knocking him over and then one for hitting them..." He tried to break the tension but Louie acted as if he lost his mind.

"Fuck the game," Louie said. He picked up another rock. With his knuckles white from the grip on the rock, he pulled his arm back but only wept. As his head bobbed, Arnie watched as Louie's body teetered on the edge.

Arnie knew that if the man kept it up they'd be out of rocks soon. And if he lost his mind, then maybe a push was in order. Sure, it was a sick thought to have—pushing an innocent, living man into a horde of zombies, but these weren't normal times.

Trying to take the *high road*, Arnie wrapped his arms around Louie and pulled him back. The rock fell to the floor with a clunk.

"Louie, please. You're losing it."

Louie dropped to his ass and kept crying. Arnie always wondered what was worse than watching a woman cry when you had nothing to offer to make it stop. He found it, and it wasn't the end of the world waiting outside, it was Louie babbling like a baby.

The crying lasted ten minutes or so until Louie sucked up all his snot and put out a shaky hand towards Arnie, offering a forgiveness handshake. "I'm sorry," he said, "I haven't had a smoke in a while. Withdrawal. And those things… I just think about all the people I know out there. Are they dead? Are they walking again, but as zombies?"

"You're the one who told me we'd be saved soon. We had to just hang out here…"

"I know, I know. I'm sorry. I need a cigarette. And a shot of whiskey."

"And a woman," Arnie added with a smile.

"Amen to that. But enough talk about what we can't have. You know what? I feel like something's going to happen today. Something's… changing."

Changing.

Louie ended up being right.

They continued throwing rocks but only a little at a time. Some were for fun but most were planned. They needed to hit and kill as many zombies as they could. The ones who looked the biggest. The ones looking up at them and making noise. Eventually their aim was spot on, splitting zombies heads open one rock at a time.

Then *the changing* part came.

Louie called out baseball stats ready to throw a four seam fastball. Arnie smiled but had no idea what Louie meant.

The rock flew with speed and accuracy. It spun, held its path, and was on track for a direct hit at a fat woman's forehead. Louie picked her because he was afraid if he and Arnie had to run, the fat one would fall on him and pin him.

A mere second before impact, the zombie stepped to the side.

The changing occurred.

"She moved!" Louie cried out.

"She moved," Arnie whispered.

Both men looked at each other.

The zombie moved. It saw the rock coming and not just moved but *knew* to move…

Every night before falling asleep Arnie and Louie talked. In the darkness it was easier to open up to each other. They were strangers for one thing and another, they were men. Not saying that all men can't open up, but the apocalypse doesn't sleep and any signs of weakness to the living or the dead could only harm.

On most nights, Arnie and Louie often discussed one question – *what could be worse than zombies?*

They now had their answer.

Smart zombies.

Before the rocks…

All night long they moved. They always moved. They didn't need sleep, they were dead.

For the first couple nights, Arnie had trouble sleeping. The sound of them moving, creeping always scared him. Louie told him time and time again they couldn't climb. Hell, they couldn't even see them. They were in a tree house. And not just any tree house, but the Taj Mahal of tree houses. It had windows, curtains, and even electricity. A mini fridge was tucked in the corner with some food and drinks. Considering the world was ending or may have ended by then, Louie called it "the last great discovery of our kind".

They'd been trapped for two days and figured once the food ran out if there wasn't help, they'd travel. Find survivors. Group up. Fight. Die. Whatever came first.

It was a tough adjustment, welcoming death that is. Like all of us, Arnie and Louie grew up to preserve their lives—*brush your teeth, eat vegetables, that kind of thing.* And now they stood looking out the door of the tree house at a small horde of zombies. In their minds they each imagined falling into the arms of the dead, wondering how long the pain would last. Arnie told himself it would be worth it if he was dead in ten seconds. Louie on the other hand wanted to be dead before being touched.

"Ahh-nie, look at them." Louie put up his fingers like a gun and pretended to shoot. A couple of the zombies moaned, stepping toward the tree.

Arnie hated being called "Ahh-nie". Being named after the Terminator was cool in its day, but not so much since the real Ahh-nald traded his steel skeleton and catch phrases for politics.

"There's more coming now," Arnie said.

"They smell us," Louie said. "They smell living tissue."

That made sense. They were left in a world with more questions than answers and nobody to help sort them out. The only glimmer of hope came from a guy named Rocky they met a day before finding the tree house.

"Sons-a-bitches did it," he said.

"Who?" Louie asked.

"Gov-n-ment," Rocky said. "Playing God again."

"How?" Arnie asked.

"Boys, there are facilities across this country that would blow your mind. They try everything on everything. Who knows? Maybe they were building a disease and it was let loose. Maybe they discovered a new silent disease and unleashed it. Maybe they were playing with new weapons to try on the terrorists or people or something and messed it up. I've seen it all. Or… or maybe it was just the right time for it all to come to an end. No jobs. No money. Corporations ruling the world. Destroying the world. Pollution. Violence. Right? Christ, can't even take your garbage out anymore without runnin' the risk of getting' robbed, shot, or sumtin bad."

Rocky waved his hands.

"Nobody knows a thing?" Arnie asked.

"Only what they're told," Rocky said. "The Gov-n-ment is already working on cover ups. But then they pulled the plug. Left us to be. Hey, did you boys know that the Gov-n-ment bought land in the mid west and dug hundreds of feet into the ground and built facilities?"

"For what?" Louie asked.

"For protection. When the end came. Like this. I bet all our politicians are down there now, drinking scotch, smoking cigars, and laughing as we all die. Yup, I bet it."

A few hours later Rocky went to piss and shot himself in the head.

Such was the pressure of living in a dying world.

"Look at them Ahh-nie, coming in groups. Staring at us. Fuckers." Louie hacked and spit. A green ball of spit and booger shot down like a missile and splat on one of the zombies head.

The creature didn't even care. It kept its eyes locked on Arnie and Louie.

"I don't like this Lou."

"Don't worry about them. They'll move on."

"How do you know that?"

"I have an idea. We can chase them out. Or at least have fun trying."

Arnie watched as Louie walked to the back of the tree house. The tree holding the wooden structure was the most perfect "tree house tree" he'd ever seen. It split about fifteen feet off the ground and the branches opened and curled up making the perfect spot for a tree house. Not a man of faith since he was ten and got mad at a priest for rubbing dirt on his head on Ash Wednesday, Arnie wondered if the tree house was there on purpose, you know, for a bigger purpose.

"Look at these babies," Louie called out. He stood up holding rocks.

"Rocks?"

"Rocks," Louie said nodding. "We're going to bomb the fuckers until they leave. Some of these in here look big enough to break open their heads. So they'll die."

Arnie walked over and there was a cedar chest filled with rocks. Hundreds, maybe even thousands. All shapes and sizes.

"Looks like someone prepared for war."

"You know kids man," Louie said, "probably had a problem with bullies or people trying to get into his tree house. So he had protection. Smart kid."

"I'm glad he did it," Arnie said grabbing the biggest rock he could find. It was slightly pointed at one end. "I'm going for gold on the first try."

"Rock n' roll brother," Louie said pointing to the door. "Nothing else to do, right? Shit, when I think about that I laugh. All those years I whined about not having a break or time to myself. Now look. I'd give anything to climb in the driver's seat of a truck and pick up other peoples garbage, you know?"

"That's how life works I guess. Grass ain't always greener, right?"

"Guess not."

Arnie closed one eye and judged the best he could.

Louie was quiet and fidgety. He hadn't a smoke in four days and it drained him. He thought about Rocky. When he went to take a piss, he had a pack of cigarettes in his breast pocket. When they found him missing half his head, somehow the cigarettes had fallen out and were in a puddle of blood. Louie considered grabbing the pack but he didn't want to look too desperate. He wished now he grabbed the pack.

"Okay," Arnie said, "bombs away..."

He dropped the rock. It was dead on. The tip hit and cracked open the skull of a zombie. It was a tall man, lanky, wearing a black suit. He was already missing an arm and an eye. The rock destroyed most of its head and snapped its neck back. The zombie fell in a pile of dead again flesh and bone. It twitched a few times and was gone.

"Shit Ahh-nie," Louie said, "you should head up Special Ops and save the world."

"One rock at time," Arnie said. "You try it."

Louie stood poised pretending to be a pitcher on the mound. "Counts three-two, runners on first and second take their leads. The wind up... and..." Louie threw the rock at a woman. Her head was tilted and bobbed; she had no idea why she was there. Just another mindless follower. In some ways they were so much like the living, only now they feasted on flesh too. The rock hit her mouth. It was smaller than Arnie's bomb but the damage was extensive. Blood and teeth sailed through the air as her head snapped back and she fell over. The rock tore a gaping hole where her mouth was, leaving nothing but a moving tongue.

"Dead?" Louie asked.

"Nah, I think you broke her neck."

The woman's eyes and tongue moved. She tried to make noise but it sounded more gargled than noise because of the blood. Her others limbs completely lifeless.

"I think we have a new game here Ahh-nie. I really do. We should keep score."

"Yeah, set up a system. Ten points for a kill."

"Five if you break their neck."

"Three if you knock them over."

"One if you hit them."

"Works for me," Arnie said.

After the changing...

Arnie was the one who had to restore order in the tree house. He and Louie used up half the rocks already. They were throwing them not with rage but pure confusion. They aimed and the zombies moved.

They dodged the rocks.

No matter what Arnie and Louie did, the zombies knew it was coming.

They changed their throws. They changed speeds. They threw two at a time, three at a time, even four at a time. They even came up with a plan, a fake out. Arnie wound up to throw a rock and Louie hid off to the side. Just as Arnie was about to release, Louie jumped out and threw his instead. The zombies should have had their eyes on Arnie but they were able to spot the fake out and move.

"I thought zombies were stupid," Arnie said.

"I guess that shit is just in books," Louie said.

"No more throwing rocks. We can't waste anything else."

Louie dropped the rock in his hand. He pointed down at a zombie. "You were gonna get that one. Your lucky day I guess."

The zombie pointed back at Louie. "Lu-hy," it called out.

Arnie couldn't believe his eyes and ears. The creatures were staring so long they were picking up on things. They were... learning. "This is bad," he whispered. "What if nobody else knows about this? What if the Government is trying to help but can't because they don't know. What if no help comes?"

"Help'll be here Ahh-nie, don't worry. And if not, we move out."

"Move out? How? They're not going anywhere. You said they'd get bored and leave. But look at them all..."

Louie looked and for the first time he realized every zombie within viewing distance, maybe a hundred of so, were all looking at the tree house. Not in the general direction of the tree house, but right at the opening where Arnie and Louie stood. When they first came, the zombies were mindless, looking off into space. Sometimes they looked at the tree house but there was no emotion behind it. Now, as Louie made eye contact with the zombies, he could almost feel them.

"This is very bad," Louie said.

"We should get out of here soon," Arnie added.

"No worries, I already have a plan."

Before Arnie could inquire, there was a sound.

An engine.

As the sound grew, a vehicle came into view.

"Look it!" Louie cried out. He dove at Arnie and hugged him. Then he jumped back. "Sorry man, I'm not... you know, like that. Not that I'm not okay with it, but you know. I just... you're kind of my best friend right now, you know?"

"Hug away," Arnie said, smiling.

It wasn't just any vehicle, but a large SUV. It rolled up the street and came to a stop a few hundred feet away from the tree house. Some of the zombies looked but then turned back to keep their eyes on Arnie and Louie. A person poked out from the sunroof of the vehicle and began to signal with his hands.

"See?" Louie said, "they must know the zombies are smart."

The passenger door opened and a man came out. He was in street clothes and had a gun in each hand. He wasted no time taking shots at the nearest zombies. Headshots, of course, splattering skull and brains everywhere.

"Not smart enough to dodge a bullet," Louie said. He was smiling and cheering like a little kid watching his favorite wrestler winning the world title.

Arnie wasn't convinced yet. Humans couldn't dodge bullets either. And for that matter, why weren't the other zombies attacking? They were smart enough to watch Louie and Arnie. They were smart enough to dodge the rocks. They were smart enough to mimic Louie. But they weren't hording against the man just feet from them?

Something was wrong. Very wrong.

"Once he pops them all, we're free," Louie said.

As Arnie thought about it, *the changing* came back again. And the answer to the question *what could be worse than zombies?* was answered again… the answer was no longer *smart zombies* but rather zombies that *become smart. Adapt. Learn. Kill…*

The man with guns was just far enough away from the SUV that when the three man zombie horde came out of a large bush, he couldn't run. They ambushed him perfectly, flanking on all sides, flustering the man. He didn't have a chance to fire his weapon; he was too focused on moving forward. The two from the sides waved their hands and yelled, distracting the man from the one coming from behind. It grabbed the man and with a violent move, the zombie tore open the man's neck. He was dead before his knees touched the ground.

The driver's door opened on the SUV and before that man could climb out, two more zombies came out of the bush and pulled him from the vehicle. They tore his throat and chest to pieces in seconds.

Adapt.

Learn.

Kill.

Louie had his hands over his mouth. He shook. Arnie was in shock of the sight, but inside, he wasn't all that surprised. He felt something brewing outside but he would have never predicted that. The zombies heard or sensed the SUV coming and formed a plan. An attack plan.

"They're getting smarter," Arnie said. "Louie, listen. We have to get out of here. They're getting smarter. Zombies." He stared out at the zombies. His look was that of shock but he was in complete control of himself. He knew what to do next.

As a human, stability feels great. Knowing the little things are in place. Comfort. It's about comfort. Even for those who don't believe in comfort and aren't afraid to step out of the box and live. They still have it, no matter what they say. They still have something to hold faith in, even if it is the adventure of life itself.

The sad part was the tree house had become a home for Louie. Maybe he shouldn't have let his emotions dangle free like he did, but he was up against the end of the world and forced to quit smoking. Louie had a built in need for comfort. And that comfort was going to be abandoned. Again.

"Louie? What's the plan?"

Arnie was the same as Louie but able to hide it. He found his parents dead, not because of age but zombies. He considered them somewhat lucky; their necks were eaten all the way through so there was no chance of them coming back. Louie had found him on the front porch, dazed. Louie took him in, helped him. They were strangers a few days ago but now Arnie trusted his life with Louie.

"Louie?" he asked again.

Louie finally turned his head. "They're smiling at me Ahh-nie. They know we're nervous."

Arnie didn't want to hear that. "Can we get out of here?"

"Yeah, we're fine, I have a plan." Louie pushed away from the door and walked towards the chest with the rocks.

"More rocks?" Arnie asked.

"Well, some for the road, right? We don't have any other weapons right now."

"Are we climbing down into them?"

"No, I'm not that crazy. Not yet. There's a trap door. I noticed it the first night we were here. I went to sit down and felt the boards jump a little. Here, look." Louie pushed the chest out of the way and sure enough, there was a secret door. The gold hinges were the only thing that gave it away. The rest of it perfectly blended in to the floor of the tree house. "When the board jumped, I moved the chest and voila. Figured it would make a good way out."

Arnie smiled.

"And if you didn't take note, there's a fence separating us from them."

That was something Arnie didn't notice. But it was true. They had climbed up the ladder at the front of the tree. A tall red fence was built right against the back of the tree. The fence ran the length of the property, keeping a barrier between them and the zombies. It wasn't a safe barrier, but enough to give them a chance to run.

Louie felt until he was able to get under the secret door. He lifted it. "Son of a bitches!"

"What's wrong Louie?"

"They're here too."

Arnie looked and sure enough, there were zombies. Only three though.

"I like these chances better," Louie said.

"Me too," Arnie said. "I just wonder how smart these things really are..."

A clunking sound came from behind the two men. They both looked and saw the ladder shaking.

"Help," Louie whispered, "help's here."

They moved back to the front of the tree house to find the complete opposite of help. It was more like hell.

The zombies were climbing the ladder. Hand over hand, rung by rung.

"They're smart," Louie said.

Arnie didn't waste time thinking about it. The ladder was hooked into the tree house. He fought and was able to get it loose enough to shake.

"Louie, help me."

Together they shook the ladder until it unhooked from the tree. Then they pushed the ladder back and it slammed against the ground along with the three zombies still trying to climb on it.

"Who's the smart one now?" Louie asked smiling.

He raised his hand to give Arnie a high five when they heard, "one now" in a rough voice.

They turned and a zombie was in the tree house.

Arnie sped into action. He grabbed a rock and smashed the creature knocking it back until it fell down the secret door to the ground.

"What's happening?" Louie asked.

"They're planning their attack..."

More noise came from the outside.

Arnie checked the front, zombies were climbing the fence and tree. They moved with accuracy, they knew what they were doing.

Louie stood over the secret door that wasn't so secret anymore. Zombies were piling up and climbing.

"They trapped us," Arnie said.

Louie closed the secret door knowing that only bought a few seconds. He looked into the chest and there were plenty of rocks to try and fight with but of course this was a numbers game. Two or three zombies, fine. Two or three hundred… Louie felt tears fill up his eyes again. He wanted a cigarette.

Arnie picked up a rock. He held it over the zombie's head that was a few feet from getting to the tree house. His eyes then scanned out, looking at the hundreds of zombies coming now. They were appearing out of nowhere. All coming for a meal. A living meal.

Arnie dropped the rock back to the floor.

He had a final answer to the question… *what could be worse than zombies?*

Zombies that are smarter than you.

13 Weapons for the Zombiepocalypse
by RC Murphy

The Zombie Survival Crew™ is concerned about the preparedness of all our crew members and felt the anthology would be incomplete without information designed to help in the event of a zombie apocalypse. This article prepared by Zombie Survival Crew™ Orange Brigade Commander RC Murphy discusses the merits of various types of methods for dealing with zombies when faced with a horde. Of course it helps to know what type of zombie you're dealing with to assist you in selecting the *BEST* weapon to aid in your defense.

☠   ☠   ☠   ☠   ☠

13. Explosives
Zombies are pack animals, much like hyenas looking for scraps to feed on. If you find yourself surrounded, toss a grenade into the crowd and run like hell. For more strategic use, lay out a few claymore mines. These use a remote detonator and keep you out of biting distance. Explosives are very handy. However, we do not suggest flinging a vial of nitroglycerin at a pack of zombies. That's just asking for trouble.

12. Salt
Should you be faced with a zombie that has been created by magical means, the easiest and best way to deal with them is with salt. Magic practitioners use salt as a cleansing and protective agent during rituals. In the case of zombies, you must pelt them with it, or put it in their mouth

to break the connection with their creator. Salt water works easiest for this. Squirt guns, anyone?

11. Machete
This weapon has a short, sharp blade that makes it easy for anyone to wield. Put enough strength behind a blow with a machete and it should cut deep enough to destroy a zombie's brain. If not, aim for the neck then stomp on the zombie's head when it hits the dirt.

10. Samurai Sword
Research shows the Samurai sword to be one of the most effective weapons in *Left 4 Dead 2*. The lightweight blade is razor sharp and slices through zombie skulls like warm butter. A note on swords: lightweight blades are made for stabbing and creating deep wounds. Heavier broadswords are made to hack and bludgeon. For zombie-slaying purposes we recommend a lighter Asian-style blade.

9. Whatever is lying around
Inevitably you will find yourself without a weapon and cornered by the undead. Look around to see what you can find. Ideal "junk" weapons are: lead pipes, 2x4s, a crowbar... anything with some weight to it will crack a zombie's skull on the first or second swing.

8. Chainsaw
Who doesn't dream of wading into a crowd of zombies with a chainsaw in hand? Okay, maybe some of you don't. But here at the ZSC we encourage ideas like that. In *The Evil Dead*, Ash proved just how useful a chainsaw can be in a fight. We're not suggesting it as a replacement for your hand, though.

7. Cricket Bat
One of the best ways to incapacitate a zombie is to bash its skull in. *Shaun of the Dead* introduced us to the idea of using a cricket bat for this purpose. The flatter shape gives the wielder more surface area utilize, making it more efficient (and cooler looking) than a baseball bat.

6. Electricity
Human bodies react poorly to electricity, dead or alive. Some breeds of zombie may not keel over from a jolt, but it will debilitate them long

enough for you to damage the brain. In *Land of the Dead* they utilize electric fences to keep the undead out of the city. Snipers pick off zombies from a safe distance once they are caught in the fence.

5. A go-go dancer with machinegun leg

This weapon will be difficult to obtain. However, if you do find someone like Cherry Darling from *Planet Terror* cherish her ability to hike a leg and take out the hoard of zombies on your tail. If you cannot locate someone with this "talent", a machinegun on its own will suffice.

4. Flamethrower

Unless you want to burn down your Safe Haven, we suggest using a flamethrower strictly outdoors. Zombies disposed of via fire will wander around until their brains are ignited and destroyed. This makes them a huge fire hazard. Know your environment. Do not use a flamethrower near a gas station or propane tank. Ka-Boom!

3. Ax

Slightly heavier than a sword, the ax is all business when it comes to zombie slaying. The heavy blade will do all of the work for you and easily cleave a zombie's head in twain. An ax is also a necessary tool to keep you well supplied with firewood. We like multipurpose weapons.

2. Crossbow/compound bow

In instances where stealth is necessary, we suggest using a crossbow or compound bow. The walkers in *The Walking Dead* were drawn by sound, making this weapon a must. The other benefit of a bow is that the arrows can be retrieved and reused. Bullets and explosives lack this handy feature.

1. Shotgun

Last, but certainly not least, we recommend a simple shotgun. Few weapons will do the same amount of damage as one blast from a shotgun. The weight of the weapon also makes it an ideal bludgeoning tool if a zombie gets too close. This is your boomstick, use it and live to see another sunrise.

Crunch Time
by Maria Kelly

Four high-school friends have educated themselves on zombie lore by playing a RPG game they've invented. They never dreamed they'd have to put their skills developed in the game to use, but an outbreak of the zombie virus forces their hand. While the town runs amok, they decide to meet in one of their game's *locations* and make a final stand. The creator of the rule book, Jimmy, goes to retrieve it, Danny is sent to buy weapons, items a teenager could legally buy, while the ringleader, Joey, and Travis, whose father has fallen victim, stay behind to plan their defense and eventual escape.

Crunch Time brings you into the world of RPG and twitter, something near and dear to the Zombie Survival Crew's heart, and takes you through the chilling choices which have to be made during a zombie attack.

About the author:

Maria Kelly lives in Pinellas Park, Florida. She's had stories and poems published in anthologies and online. She writes about talking dragons, an alien/shape-shifting/serial-killer spider, zombies, twisted fairy tales, and a basement dweller who makes Cthulhu look like a Care Bear. In her spare time she drinks coffee (lots of it), plays Mah-Jongg, and attends college in the hopes of someday being able to wear a tee-shirt that reads: "I Teach Banned Books." Visit her website at: http://mariakellyauthor.com or follow her on Twitter—@mkelly317.

When the zombies come, she is going to hack off their heads with a broadsword and feed 'em to the gators.

Crunch Time

Joey Costello wiped the dust from the cheddar puffs onto his jeans and leaned forward to stare at the brightly lit computer monitor. It was his older brother David's hand-me-down computer: the one that looked like some fucked-up futuristic space-lamp.

He waited for his tweeps to respond. He watched as line upon line in the stream scrolled past, none of them from his crew.

"C'mon, dudes, damn!" he yelled, banging his fist down on the desk.

He cursed again as a whole load of tweets went sailing by, and he had to scroll down to make sure he didn't miss one from his friends.

"Oh, man, we SO need our own hashtag." He made a mental note to spring this bit of brilliant wisdom on his tweeps when they got on line. Where the hell where they, anyway?

He was half-way through the tweets when the auto-refresh kicked in and zoomed a hundred more tweets past his eyes.

"Aw, goddammit!" He swore again, but not too loudly. His mom had begun tolerating him dropping the 'F-bomb' but she'd tear his ass up if she heard him using that word. Not that his mother was particularly religious, but Aunt Lois was, and Aunt Lois was always over at their place these days since Uncle Reggie passed.

Finally, his trembling finger stilled on the scroll button as he read the message:

2ndTimeDead: RT @ZombieHuntR666 holla back mah boyz when u online. | | I'm on, Z.

"Yes!" Joey whispered as he typed and waited for his message to appear onscreen:

ZombieHuntR666: @2ndTimeDead it is as we feared, brotha!!!

He waited for 2ndTimeDead's reply:

2ndTimeDead: @ZombieHuntR666 I know that's right, bro! Saw 2 on way home from Crosswalk. Scared the fuck outta me. What do we do?

ZombieHuntR666: @2ndTimeDead don't fuckin panic. that's the most important thing. don't fuckin panic. u been readin these other tweets?

2ndTimeDead: @ZombieHuntR666 4realz! Both #zombieapocalypsenow and #realzombiegeddon are TT'ing! WTF? They're all over the world! WTF? #whatthefuck

ZombieHuntR666: @2ndTimeDead i said don't panic dude. oh shit! SHIT! brb...

2ndTimeDead: @ZombieHuntR666 Joey! WTF? Joey???????

2ndTimeDead: @ZombieHuntR666 Joey i'm fuckin comin over there in about 3 minutes if you don't tweet me the fuck back!!!!

2ndTimeDead: @ZombieHuntR666 4realz mofo! I aint playin! Are you ok? Joey i swear to god you better not be playin!!!!!!!!!

ZombieHuntR666: @2ndTimeDead damn dude it was just my mom.

2ndTimeDead: @ZombieHuntR666 You scared the fuck outta me asshole!!! I thought one of them got you.

ZombieHuntR666: @2ndTimeDead LOL sorry dude :P dude, we need our own hashtag. going thru these tweets is bullshit.

2ndTimeDead: @ZombieHuntR666 Dude, how about #oakleafHSzombies?

Sometimes Danny surprised Joey with a flash of brilliance. Since the zombie virus outbreak in their town seemed to have started at their school, #oakleafHSzombies was the perfect hash.

ZombieHuntR666: @2ndTimeDead Danny Patton you're a fuckin genius! that's brilliant i swear to god.

At the thought of his school, Joey's hands dropped off the keyboard.

How many Oak Leaf High School students had already been turned? He shook himself alert and grabbed the keyboard again. "I need to chill the fuck out." He DM'ed his other two friends to inform them about the hashtag:

ZombieHuntR666: dudes. tweet me and Danny on hashtag #oakleafHSzombies. we have GOT to get together and do something about these fuckin zombies!!!!

Joey tried their cell phones one more time, but neither one of them was answering. Joey saw a new g-mail stating he had a DM from Travis Bower, a.k.a. @phath3adX. He opened his Twitter DM.

phath3eadX: They killed my dad, Joey! WTF?

Joey sat and stared at the screen for several minutes, stunned. What the hell do you say to something like that? Another DM popped into view:

crunchtime7: Joey, ppl are running around everywhere, zombies attacking. We need to get the hell out of here!

They'd invented their own RPG zombie game just for fun. The places they met and exercises that they had to perform to gain points, well, that was all part of the game. This was no game. Now, the shit was for real, and Joey had no idea what to do. It might have been a good idea to get some of the other kids at school in on the game, then they'd have had more people to help in fighting the zombies. But none of them had for a moment ever thought seriously that there might one day be a real zombie apocalypse! Besides, they weren't popular with the other kids at Oak Leaf High. Joey thought it might have something to do with the fact that the four of them were total geeks.

He shook himself violently, and focused. He typed the DM's quickly, telling them where to meet. He didn't bother to try and comfort Travis. What do you say to someone whose dad has become brain food for a hungry zombie?

Joey got up from his desk and grabbed his jacket and book bag. On the way out of his house, he stopped in his kitchen and loaded up on food from the refrigerator and pantry and then cursed himself for not telling the other boys to do the same.

#

"Man, this is some fucked up shit!" Danny paced up and down the length of the old boxcar.

Joey watched him nervously. He'd wanted to tell him to stop, it was driving him crazy, but he didn't say anything. Joey diverted his attention back to a map of the city which was spread out on the grimy old milk crate in front of him. He sat on a sturdier crate and traced a green highlighted line with his index finger. They'd used the map countless times for their game, but now it was for real. They were alone in the boxcar, called "location 24" in the game. Travis Bower and Jimmy Posey, @crunchtime7, had not shown up yet. It was two hours since he'd sent the messages. And neither of the boys answered their cell phones. Where were they?

Joey decided needless worrying wasn't going to help matters. They needed a plan.

"Danny, stop pacing and bring me your tablet," he said.

"Why?"

"Just do it," Joey said, Danny's anxiety bothered him. This was not the time to panic. That time, Joey knew, would come soon enough: probably staring into a zombie's lifeless eyes.

Danny went to his book bag and brought Joey the tablet computer. He stood next to Joey and watched as his friend logged on the internet and found Superpages for their hometown.

"Whatcha lookin' for?" Danny asked.

"We're gonna need some weapons," Joey replied,

Danny jumped and made a fist-pump. "Oh, hells yeah! I want a fuckin' AK47, dude!"

Joey rolled his eyes at his friend. "Pffft! We're not gonna be able to get heavy artillery like that, asswiper! We're kids!"

"So what are you thinking?" Danny asked. He watched as Joey pulled up addresses for several local hardware stores and an auto supply store.

"We need to make a list. Do you have any paper?" Joey asked.

Danny hurried back over to his book bag, and rummaged through it. "You didn't bring any paper?"

"I brought food, dammit! Thought we'd need that a little bit more, if we have to stay here."

"You mean we won't be able to go home?" Danny asked, wide-eyed, as he brought Joey his composition notebook from English class. It was practically unused.

"Not if the zombies get to our families. I haven't heard from my mom, and I keep calling her."

Joey tore a sheet from the notebook and began writing items down.

"A tire iron?" Danny asked.

"An incredibly useful weapon, and one we'll be able to buy."

"We can't lug around a heavy-ass tire iron everywhere?" Danny argued.

"We're not going to lug them around everywhere, you moron. We're going to bring them back here. If we're out there, and running from the zombies, we can come back here and make a final stand. And they're not that heavy."

"Were tire irons on the game list?" Danny asked. The Crunch Time RPG game was the brainchild of Jimmy Posey, which is why his Twitter name was @crunchtime7. They had an elaborate list of weapons as well as locations where the four would meet and do mock battle. They each took turns being zombies and squad leader. They had escape routes drawn on the map in different shades of highlighter. There were various scenarios written on index cards, one of which was drawn at the beginning of each game. The boys never actually used any real items as weapons in the game, but had a system of "calling out" which weapon they were using for each play of the game.

"Yes, but I don't think we ever used them. Anything that can knock a zombie's brains out is a weapon. Can you think of anything?" Joey asked.

"We need the game rules. Baseball bats are on the list, that's all I know." Danny replied. And they had a few baseball bats tucked away in the boxcar. They'd brought them there so they could play baseball in the empty lot behind the abandoned train yard.

"And machetes," Joey said, scribbling.

"Where in hell are we going to get machetes?" Danny protested. "We need to contact Crunch and have him bring the rules. Couldn't hurt to go over some of that stuff."

Joey started to criticize him, but then he realized that the notebook Posey had made not only had the game rules and weapons list, it also had useful information gleaned from the pages of every zombie survival guide and website they could find, along with the information they got from playing Resident Evil at each others houses. Joey reached for his cellphone, but it rang in his hand, startling him so badly that he nearly dropped it.

"Whoa!" Danny said. "That was fuckin' prophetic!"

It was Posey.

Joey answered it. "Where the fuck are you, dude?"

"Fifth and Terrace. Guy, this is more serious than we thought. There's zombies everywhere downtown. The Crosswalk, Edgewater Mall, you name it!"

"We know that. Get your ass here as quick as you can. We're forming a plan and we need the book."

"The book?"

"The game book! Do you have it on you?"

"No, shit! It's at home. You want me to go get it?"

"Yes! All that survival stuff is in there. We're gonna need that shit!" Joey yelled into the phone. "Is your family okay? Have you heard from Travis?"

"My dad is still missing. My mom cries all the time. But my older sister and brother are taking care of her. I'm still hopin' he's okay and just out killin' zombies. Missing is better than dead. Like Travis' dad."

"Yeah," Joey said.

"Yeah," Jimmy reiterated. "I'll get to the yard as soon as I get the book. I gotta get outta this area. Haven't seen any undead for a little while, but it's like, weird downtown. Dead. It's givin' me the fuckin' creeps."

"Okay, see ya. Hurry up!" Joey hung up the phone. Danny was looking at him expectantly. "Do you have any cash?"

"I have my debit card. There's a good bit on it, but I pulled out three-hundred bucks earlier today. Thought the ATM's might go down, like they do sometimes in a disaster."

Joey smiled. "You're fuckin' brilliant. If you weren't a guy and didn't have breath like a pig's ass, I'd kiss you!"

Danny grimaced. "You so would not, dude!"

Joey smiled and threw a mock-punch at Danny's shoulder.

"Just kidding," Joey said. He pointed at an address on the tablet. "Go to this hardware store, and pick up what you can from this list. Enough for the four of us. Whatever you can afford."

Danny grabbed the list and started to reach for the tablet. Joey pulled it away from his grasp. "I need this to look up some other stuff. Leave it here with me. I won't break it, I swear."

Danny nodded, turned around and left the boxcar.

#

After Danny left, Joey decided to practice swinging a baseball bat. He tried to keep the bat at head level and imagined knocking a putrid zombie's head clear over the Green Monster at Fenway Park for a Grand Slam. He stayed in the boxcar, afraid he'd see a zombie if he ventured too far outside.

After about thirty minutes of bat practice his arms got tired, so he went and sat back down on the crate, accessing the web again on Danny's tablet.

His breath caught and he gulped when he logged on Twitter.

brainpecker93: @ZombieHuntR666 hey you...you don't know me, but I know u. #oakleafHSzombies

notreallydead: @brainpecker93 @ZombieHuntR666 we know who you are, joey. #oakleafHSzombies

Joey scrolled down until he'd found the first one, then he moved up through the tweets, becoming more perplexed with each one. Who the hell were these guys? He scrolled, reading each message from them—still wondering—when his eyes froze on the following tweets:

notreallydead: @ZombieHuntR666 @2ndTimeDead @phatH3adX know who you ALL are. how's ur fucking daddy travis? tee hee. #oakleafHSzombies

brainpecker93: @notreallydead @phatH3eadX his daddy was delicious...#nomnomnom #oakleafHSzombies

notreallydead: @brainpecker93 hate it when ur food bites back. LOL! #oakleafHSzombies

Shit! They're zombies? How could that be? Joey didn't know what to make of it. He thought that zombies were supposed to be mindless automatons on a continual hunt for a McBrain Sandwich. He watched as the stream jumped upwards, indicating a new tweet. He went to it and his heart felt like a popsicle.

brainpecker93: @notreallydead @ZombieHuntR666 @2ndTimeDead @phatH3adX we're coming to get you...bwahahahaha! #NotLD #oakleafHSzombies

Then another jump:

notreallydead: @ZombieHuntR666 @2ndTimeDead @phatH3adX BOOO!

CLANK CLANK!!!

Joey dropped the tablet to the floor as a metallic stomp and a shadow fell on him through the open doorway of the boxcar. He jumped up and ran to the corner where the baseball bats were and grabbed one, swinging to face the new arrival.

"Jesus, Joey! It's me!" Travis cried. He walked into the boxcar, his motorcycle boots, his "shit-kickers" as he liked to called them, clanging on the floor.

Joey relaxed and went back to the crate, praying that Danny's tablet computer wasn't busted. Danny would kick his ass, for sure. He picked it up and looked it over, front-to-back. Somehow, it didn't even get a scratch. Joey let out the breath he'd been holding in a long sigh, hoping that Travis didn't notice his trembling hands.

"You scared the shit outta me," he said.

Travis walked over and pulled another old crate up to sit across from Joey. "Man, it's fuckin' madness out there!"

"Yeah, it is," Joey said. "But we're gonna make it, don't you worry. I sent Danny out to get some weapons and Jimmy's goin' to his house to get the book. We're gonna be okay."

"I got the book," Travis said, pulling it out of a worn Cincinnati Reds back-pack.

Joey looked up at him in surprise. He frowned at the dark circles under his friends red-rimmed eyes.

Travis noticed how Joey was looking at him and shifted slightly, thumbing open the book. "Kept trying to call Posey but he never answered, so I went over to his house and got it."

"His mom let you in? Just like that?"

"Yes. Why wouldn't she?" Travis looked at him in confusion.

Joey shook his head. "Because. Anybody could be one of them now. You can't just go trusting people anymore without first checking."

"Do I look like a zombie?"

"No, but..." Joey started, but Travis interrupted.

"My dad is."

"Holy shit!" said Joey.

"I saw him. He was shuffling down Piney Street toward the mall. His left arm from the elbow down had been chewed off."

"Dammit! Jimmy was in that area when he called me! I hope he's got enough sense to avoid him if he sees him." Or kill him, Joey thought.

"Dude, I hate to say it, but I hope it doesn't come down to me having to kill my own dad. I don't think I could do it!"

Travis looked away and Joey thought he must be fighting back tears again. He reached out and patted his friends back, not knowing what else to do, then stood up and walked to the corner of the boxcar where their baseball stuff was. They had about fifteen baseballs in various states of use: some brand new, some worn and frayed but still good for playing catch. He smiled and pulled out his phone. He turned around and walked back to the crate-seats, texting as he went.

"I'm gonna have Danny swing by the sporting goods store on his way back. I got an idea for another weapon." Joey said. His eyes lit up with the spark of sweet fucking idea.

"Yeah, what?" Travis asked.

When Joey told him, Travis grinned.

He turned to the weapons section of the game book and fished inside his backpack for a pen.

"Did you bring what I asked you to?" Joey asked. Travis reached in his bag and pulled out the best weapon of all. Numero Uno on the list of weapons.

"Awesome!" Joey cried, taking it from his friend's hand and caressing it lovingly.

The boys began discussing the plan.

#

They were in the middle of laying the ground-work to what they were dubbing the "distract-and-destroy" plan when Joey suddenly remembered the unknown tweeters. He questioned Travis.

"No idea who they are," the boy said. "But brainpecker..." Travis paused, thinking. "I don't like it."

"What?" Joey asked.

Travis shrugged. "Nothing." Then he looked really pensive, like he might be thinking of his dad again, so Joey let the matter drop. He wondered vaguely if Mr. Bower had been one of the ones sending the messages. Travis's dad was like, forty-years-old, but still, even old people like parents knew how to use Twitter. Still...zombies on Twitter? Every zombie movie, T.V. show, book, or video game they'd ever watched, read, read, or played, from *28 Days Later* to *Zombie Tycoon* all portrayed the undead as mindless, shuffling hordes. It was a scary thought.

"What if these are smart zombies?" Joey asked.

"No fuckin' way!" Travis cried. "That defies logic!"

Joey thought about it, and the more he thought about it, the more uneasy he became. Maybe they weren't smart zombies, but what if they didn't become completely mindless when they transformed?

"Listen," Travis said. "I bet those tweeters are Johnson and Haynes."

He was referring to Tommy Johnson and Al Haynes, two bullies they went to Oak Leaf High School with. Joey considered this. It would be just like those two assholes to do this. But how did they know their Twitter names? Or about the hashtag they were using? Joey brooded on these questions silently but did not mention his concerns to Travis.

They both looked up suddenly as Danny entered the boxcar, arms full of supplies. He was gasping and out of breath.

"Wish one of you dickheads would come and help me with this crap!" he sighed. He put down the bags he was carrying and grimaced at them both. "There's plenty more. Hop to it!"

The three boys ventured outside to unload the trunk of Danny's 2001 Chevy Cavalier. Danny was the only one of the group to pass his driver's test so far, and since he had a car he was always being called for rides.

There was also a pepperoni pizza from Vino's on the front passenger's side seat. Danny brought that and a two-liter of cola into the boxcar. They ate pizza and drank the cola from a supply of old cups they'd scrounged from the backs of cupboards at their homes ages ago. While they ate, they went over the plan.

Joey talked excitedly as he showed them what he had in mind. He loaded one of the sling-shots Danny purchased at the sporting goods store with a baseball and fired it across the boxcar. The ball hit with a tremendous CRACK and ricocheted back, Travis had to duck to avoid being beaned.

"Whoa!" Danny cried. "I thought you were crazy when you texted me to pick up sling-shots. They make a terrible weapon against zombies. But this is fucking brilliant!"

"No, the sling-shot itself won't kill 'em," Joey agreed. "But it should knock 'em down long enough to do the rest of the job."

"Sweet!" Travis proclaimed.

They took turns practicing with the sling in different areas of the boxcar. Without a target, there was no way to tell if each of them were actually any good wielding it, but in the end they all agreed that Danny and Joey seemed to be the best. Which left Travis to handle the "destroy" end of things. And that was logical, since it was his dad's weapon he had brought with him. He'd practiced with it many times before.

They also had a back-up plan, in case Travis failed to dispatch the zombie. The two new tire irons were resting against the back wall of the boxcar. Joey had resisted getting four of every item they might need. They had the baseball bats, tire irons, sling-shots, plus two axes. And hopefully Travis wouldn't let them down when it was time to play his part.

Joey looked at his watch. "Where the HELL is Posey?"

The other two boys shook their heads. The looked over at the beat-up red milk crate that Joey had used earlier as a desk to study the book and map of the town. On it sat a paper plate holding a couple slices of pizza and a cup of soda. They glanced at the open door of the boxcar and saw that daylight was fading. They'd been so caught up in planning and practicing with the sling-shots that they'd forgotten about their friend.

"Call him again," Travis suggested.

Joey took his cell phone out of his pocket and flipped it open.

Then, they heard it.

A noise that sounded like the clinking of the gate leading into the old train-yard. But the gate always stood open. None of them had closed it...

The boys looked at each other, horrified, as the truth of what they heard dawned on them. The gate wasn't being opened, it was being closed.

Each of them ran to different parts of the boxcar and grabbed a weapon. Joey, in a fit of nerves, ended up grabbing a baseball bat instead of a sling-shot. "Shit!" he whispered. He threw it down and grabbed one of the axes that Danny had also bought at the hardware store. He motioned to Travis, who began climbing one-handed, his weapon balanced in the crook of his other arm, up the rungs of the ladder set into the back wall of the boxcar. He climbed to the top and his head disappeared through the square opening. He pulled it back through moments later, and shook his head at Joey. He hadn't seen anything. Danny ran to the opposite corner, sling-shot in hand, and his book bag full of baseballs slung over his shoulder.

They heard footsteps approaching the boxcar. Was it only one pair of feet they heard?

"Hey guys?" the voice called.

Danny dropped the sling-shot and bag to the ground and raced toward the door. It was Posey's voice.

"DANNY, NO!!" Joey called out.

But his admonition went unheeded as Danny raced to the door of the boxcar and jumped out. Travis started to descend the ladder, but Joey called out to him:

"Stay there! I don't like this!" Joey ran over to the door and looked out into the twilight of the dead train-yard. He saw Posey embracing Danny, his head on Danny's shoulder. Then Danny slumped to the ground as Jimmy Posey looked up at Joey, his lifeless eyes locked on his...blood dripping from his mouth.

"Crunch time," Posey whispered.

Joey spun back into the boxcar, struggling not to vomit. He raced over to the corner and grabbed the sling and bag of balls, lying the axe down. That wouldn't be any use now.

"What the fuck's happening?!" Travis yelled from the top of the ladder.

"Posey's a zombie," Joey replied. "He got Danny."

"Shit," Travis said. He reached back into his own bag and pulled out one the arrows, knocking it into place in the cross-bow. "Shit," he whispered again, just loud enough for Joey to hear, as Joey slowly inched toward the door. "Be careful." Then he climbed up through the hole and onto the roof of the boxcar.

Joey made it to the door and peered outside. He didn't see Posey anywhere but Danny was still lying on the ground. He was shaking, which meant he was still alive. Or...

"Oh, fuck," Joey muttered. He tried to stop it, but tears leaked from his eyes and rolled down his cheeks. "Fuck, dude."

There was nothing for it. Joey went back inside the boxcar to where the axe was and picked it up, and looping the sling-shot around his wrist so as not to drop it, he jumped as silently as possible out of boxcar door, walked over to where his friend lay and with one swing, separated Danny's head from his body. Joey dropped the axe and leaned over, puking in the grass.

He heard a muffled groan and spun around, looking for Posey. He heard it again and, looking up, saw Travis crouched on the top of the boxcar, wiping his mouth with the back of his hand. Travis must have vomited, too.

Joey motioned at Travis, waving his arm around. Travis got the message and stood up, scanning the yard, looking for Posey. He didn't need to.

"Crunch time, Joey," the voice issued from the other side of Danny's car. "Crunch time is comin' to get you..."

Shit. Brainpecker93! And suddenly Joey remembered what Travis had shrugged off earlier. When the boys first met Jimmy Posey, Travis has teased him by calling him Pecker Brain. At the time all four of them had laughed their asses off.

"Hey Joey, did you save me Danny's brain? 'Cause I sure am hungry!" Posey stood up from behind the car and shuffled toward Joey.

Joey fumbled with the opening of the book bag, cursing as he tried to remove a baseball, backpedaling at the same time. He hoped Travis had the sight of that crossbow trained on Posey!

He fit the baseball into the cup of the sling-shot. It didn't fit perfectly, but that was hardly the point. Lead shot came with the sling-shot, but they'd all agreed that a baseball was bigger and might do more damage. Baseball players usually went down when they got beaned by a ninety mile-per-hour fastball.

Posey kept coming toward him slowly as Joey raised the sling-shot and pulled it taut. He waited until he thought Posey was close enough to hit, then released the sling.

The baseball went sailing through the air and...went wide of Jimmy's head by about three feet.

"Fuck!" Joey cried.

Posey laughed maniacally. "I'm still coming, Joey, still coming to get youuuu....hahahaha!"

Joey rummaged in the bag for another ball. The bag slid off his shoulder and hit the ground, baseballs scattering everywhere.

"Dammit!!" Joey yelled. He took a step forward to try and retrieve one of the rolling balls, then realized he was traveling right toward Posey and he backpedaled. His foot came down on a baseball and he stumbled backwards, falling on his ass.

Posey was a mere five-feet from him now and closing the distance. "You smell good," he said, sniffing the air. "I love the smell of fresh meat and brains."

Joey looked up desperately at the boxcar roof. There was no sign of Travis.

"TRAVIS!!! Where the hell are you, dude??!!"

He turned back just as Posey was leaning toward his head, teeth bared.

Joey closed his eyes and waited for death.

A sudden pffffftttt! sound and Jimmy's heavy body fell on top of him. Joey crawled out from beneath the bulk and opened his eyes. Jimmy was lying on his back, glazed eyes unmoving. An arrow was sticking through the middle of Jimmy's forehead.

Joey turned his head and saw Travis emerging from the boxcar with the crossbow. He got to his feet, red-hot anger glaring in his eyes.

"You motherfucker! He could've killed me while you..."

"I knew I couldn't hit him from the top of the roof," Travis explained. "Motherfucker? I just saved your life."

Travis grinned and the two boys broke out in laughter.

"It's time for Plan B, I think," Joey said.

"Yeah, dude," Travis agreed. "Let's get the fuck out of here."

#

They hacked Danny and Jimmy's heads to bits, making certain the brains were mush before packing the car with the food they had left and all the weapons except the crossbow, which Travis held onto like a favorite toy.

Joey wished they could have buried their friends, but there was no time. They had to get out while the getting was good.

They lingered for a bit inside the boxcar, making sure they'd gotten everything they needed.

It was getting very dark when they exited the boxcar.

"Hi, Travis."

Travis's dad was sitting on the hood of the car.

Joey saw his friends eyes go wide and remembered what Travis said earlier about not being able to kill his dad.

"You gotta do it, man. You gotta," Joey whispered.

"You don't "gotta" do anything, Travis," Mr. Bower said. "I'm not really dead, Travis. Look at me. I'm not really dead!"

The two boys looked at each other. Notreallydead.

Mr. Bower slid off the hood and came toward them. Joey suddenly regretted having put all the weapons in the car, including the sling-shot. He was completely weaponless. He nudged Travis.

"You gotta do it, Travis," Joey urged.

"I can't, dude."

"Damn right you can't!" Mr. Bower's yelled. He kept shuffling toward them, getting closer, while Travis trembled, crossbow slack in his hands.

"Goddammit, gimme that!" Joey yelled. He grabbed the crossbow and yanked an arrow from the bag slung over Travis's shoulder. He stopped. He'd only fired it once, in the Bowers backyard, with Mr. Bowers guiding him. And he'd missed the target by about ten feet. He couldn't afford to miss this time. Not by any amount. He brought the weapon up and fired.

The arrow sliced through the night and pierced Travis's dad through the throat. He went down, flopping on the ground like a hooked fish. Travis, jerking himself to awareness, ran to the car and got the axe from the backseat. He rushed over and screaming with agony, decapitated his father. He then turned the axe and crushed his father's skull with the flat of the blade.

Travis sank to the ground and began to sob. Joey walked over and put his hand on his friend's shoulder.

"C'mon, dude. Plan B."

Travis got up and the two boys got into the car, Joey on the driver's side. He'd at least had some driving lessons under his belt.

They resisted the urge to look back at the bodies.

Joey started the car and backed slowly through the gate, which was open after all.

"Travis, you had to do it," Joey said.

"I know, dude...I know."

"Another thing," Joey started as he eased the car onto the deserted back street leading away from the train-yard.

"What?" asked Travis.

"You gotta teach me how to use that fuckin' crossbow!"

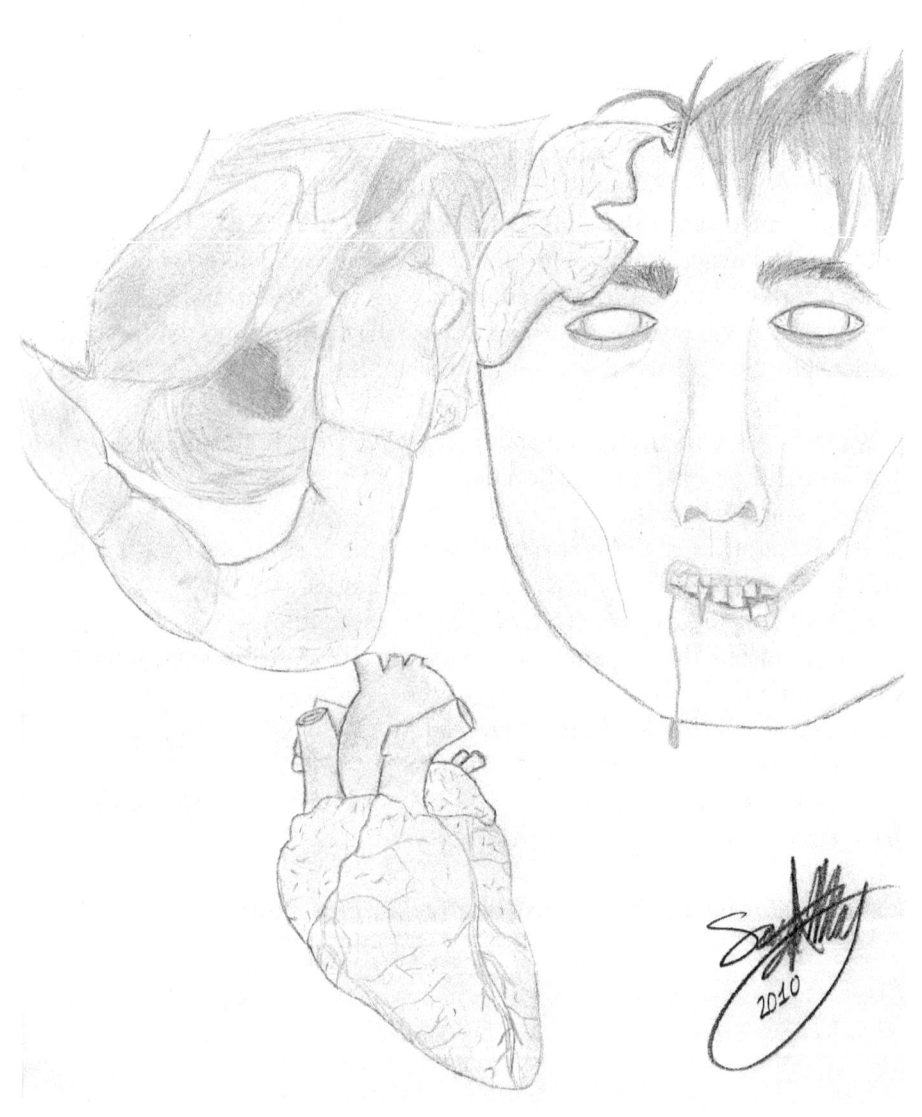

Adrian's Undead Diary
by Chris Philbrook

Adrian Ring is our intrepid hero here, having just barely survived a world consuming apocalypse of the undead. Adrian's Diary chronicles his battles with the zombie hordes and his ongoing struggle with survival. Read and understand exactly how he has lived up to this point, avoiding starvation, zombies, injuries, sickness, as well as sharing in his humor and his horror. *Adrian's Undead Diary* is an online chronicle and features stories that intersect with the happenings in the journal as well.

About the author:

Chris Philbrook is the creator and author of *Adrian's Undead Diary* (AUD). Chris has several years of experience working in game development and editing as well as writing fiction for several major game design companies. He has been published several times online, as well as multiple times in magazines related to the hobby industry. He has a business degree as well as a psychology degree.

AUD is a pet project of his that he started because he was bored at work, and always wanted to write stories about zombies. His brother from another mother Joseph Tremblay has come aboard to help make this a reality. Chris has been writing for years, and only within the last 5 or 6 years has he truly dedicated himself to spreading his work out into the real world and getting feedback and exposure.

Chris is the owner of Tier One Games LLC, his game development company. He is working on their seminal Role Playing release now, Elmoryn: The Fall of Man.

Chris lives with his lovely wife and moronic cat Brady in New Hampshire. He is an avid reader, writer, role player, miniatures game player, video game player, and part time athlete as well. Catch Chris on Twitter as @adriansdiary.

Primary weapon of choice is a Glock 17 because he likes his chances with a firearm, but when the ammunition runs dry his plan is to beat the zombies to death with his scalding wit.

Adrian's Undead Diary

September 21st.

It's pretty fucking cold out tonight. The big ass plastic thermometer on the tree outside says its 35F out tonight. I'm glad I figured out where the emergency generator is here, otherwise I would be freezing my balls off now. Despite the fact that this place was kind of a bitch to clear out, I'm glad I did it. It's got everything I need to survive for a long time.

I don't even really know where to start. It's a Tuesday today. At least I know what day it is. Someone in the main office building was wise enough to buy their calendar early this year so it'll be easy for me to keep track of the days until the end of next year. After that I guess I'll have to use some of the graph paper and make my own calendar. That's being pretty optimistic though. The way the last few months have been I'll be goddamn lucky to make Christmas, let alone next Christmas.

I decided to start writing this mainly to keep track of my daily activities and to have a way to purge my nugget. Frankly I talk to myself way too goddamn much to be mentally healthy and I was always told that writing a journal helped. Sooo... let's call this my journal. Thank God for spell check. I also realize that now is not the best time to be writing. I'm using up some of my gasoline to run the generator, which is basically a waste, and honestly having any lights on at night draws them in. Moths to a flame as the old saying goes. But I can't sleep and I've been meaning to do this for a long time now. Having the electricity back has set a fire under my ass to do this.

My name is Adrian Ring. I lived what I would now call as only a moderately successful life. I was happy, but I had pretty low standards. I had a girlfriend, I had a small condo downtown, I still have my cat (score!), and I have thus far avoided being eaten by the undead. Surprise!

There's the twist in the story. I fucking love horror movies. Like seriously. I watched well over a thousand of them and always used to plot and plan should zombies ever rise from the dead and take over the world. Irony in all that is that when the shit hit the fan it happened so fast that any kind of plan would've been almost impossible to execute.

I was at work the night it started. I used to work third shift at a private school as a dorm supervisor. It was out of the way up in the hills outside of downtown, and only had about 100 students. Over 100k a year to attend. Very elite, very snooty, and basically the best job you could ask for. I had 9 hour shifts where I basically just made sure the kids didn't run away, and had their needs taken care of. Most nights I would do maybe an hour of work. I spent the rest of the time fucking around online looking at stupid videos and screwing around on the big ole f-book. God I wish I could update my status right now. Something really witty like "hasn't been eaten yet, so is pretty stoked." Or maybe something like, "wishes he grabbed more bullets when he raided the gun store in town." I dunno. Something cool.

Anyway, I was at work when it all hit. Working nights meant I was totally alone aside from the three other overnights and the sleeping kids, so when I checked the news websites and saw the few updates about "zombie hoaxes" I laughed. After a few hours more and more popped up on other websites, but I didn't take it too seriously. After all Halloween was coming up soon I figured it was some kind of stunt to promote a new movie or TV show. It wasn't until the morning when half the day shift people didn't show that I really realized something was up.

I went home as I normally do, and nothing seemed amiss. I called my girlfriend on the short drive home and we chatted. I asked her about it and she basically said she thought it was a hoax or some stunt. She was still half asleep though, so who knows what she really saw or heard on tv. Plus she was getting ready for work herself. She was gone by the time I got home, and I never saw her again. I think she was killed at work, or maybe on the drive home from work. I'll never know. The cities are far too dangerous for me to attempt to go to, and to be honest, as much as I loved her, it scares the shit out of me when I think of getting eaten alive. If you can read this babe, I love you.

I went to bed after watching a few minutes of the news and eating a banana. I can still remember the weird vibe on the good morning shows. Kinda tense, but sort of laughing it off. I can still remember the look on the dude's face as he reported it, kinda like he was waiting for an "April fools!" to pop up on his teleprompter. Never came I guess. So I went to bed.

I slept pretty good until about 3pm. I remember distinctly waking with a start, jarred awake. It took me a few minutes to piece together what actually woke me up, but the second gunshot kinda solved that riddle. It came from outside my window in the condo complex and I knew instantly something was very wrong.

My curtains are taped right to the window frames to block out the light, so I pulled on my gym shorts and hustled downstairs to look out the glass slider on the back side of the house. The action had ended by the time I got down there, but about thirty feet from where my place is I could clearly see a dead body laying in the parking lot. Have you ever seen someone take a shotgun blast to the head? Its horrible. There's no head left to speak of, first off, and secondly the body just empties the blood out of what's left of the head. More of a neck by that point really.

The body, a woman incidentally, was lying toward my place, kinda downhill, and the blood was running into the mulch at the foot of the pine tree right behind my place. I've seen dead bodies before, I've been around violence plenty of times, but this was weird. It was in my neighborhood. You know, your sanctuary? I imagine the way I felt looking at her head-stump empty was a lot like watching your house burn down, or coming home to realize your house had been broken into. I felt violated. Anyway, I grabbed my sweatshirt, my cell phone, slipped my sandals on and sprinted out the back, dialing 911 as I went. I tripped over a root from the fucking pine tree and ate shit on the way, but I got there.

She was dead, of that there was no doubt. Her head was absolutely demolished. She was wearing a garish flowery pattern shirt that looked a lot like the kind of shirts that a pediatric nurse would wear. She definitely had pants that looked a lot like those greenish scrub pants you see nurses wearing. I made my decision. Headless shotgun woman had been a nurse only a short time ago. At that point I realized my 911 call wasn't going through. Getting the all circuits' busy bullshit, which instantly set off my oh-shit radar. My groggy ass brain finally started to put two and two together. The zombie shenanigans from last night may not have been a hoax.

I don't own a gun. My girlfriend was kinda twitchy, and she had a little bit of a temper, and I really didn't want a firearm around that cocktail. It was far too foreseeable to see me getting shot because she thought I was a robber or something. So no guns. I did however own a few very high quality swords. Competently made and purchased at a few nerd festivals over the years. I really didn't want to grab a sword and just go driving around on the outside chance that this was just a random shooting, but I knew I had to get the fuck back inside one way or the other. If this was a random shooting, the random shooter was still pretty fucking nearby and I was not in the mood to get head-stumped myself.

So I ran inside. This time I did not eat shit on the root from the pine tree, and made it inside like an Olympic sprinter. I do remember being really pissed at myself because I left the slider open and my frigging cat Otis was sitting right on the fringe watching me the time. I didn't want him to get out, as he's an inside cat. He's a Maine Coon, so he's a beefy guy, but I woulda been pissed if he got hit by a car, or shot by a psycho with a twelve gauge. Seems like a reasonable concern considering the prior events, right? Whatever dude. I love my cat. He's my homeboy.

So by then I'd tried dialing 911 like 4 times. I had the number for the police station already in my contacts so I called that line, and I got their automated response. The emergency choice just routed me to 911, and I was right back where I started. At that point I knew shit was bad. Can't be a coincidence. I hit the tv on and there it was, the EAS message. You know that irritating noise you hear when they're testing the emergency system? And very fucking rarely is there ever an emergency. I mean I guess in the Midwest when they get tornadoes, or in the south when a hurricane is coming it's more relevant than here. All we ever get is shit like "emergency snowstorm warnings," or shit like road closures or accidents.

I'll never forget the message from that day:

State and local agencies are reporting widespread attacks on citizens across the region. Authorities are advising people to stay inside, lock their doors, bar their windows and only open doors for known friends and family who respond intelligently.

That was it. No mention of a virus, aliens attacking, zombies, vampires, or any such nonsense. I mean, I know now after having seen it a few hundred times we're dealing with zombies, but that message had no info at all. For the astute horror fan though, that's when I knew it was "on." You know, as in "it's on like Donkey Kong." I tried calling my girlfriend, both on her cell phone, and at her work extension, but no dice. I'm pretty fortunate in that I don't panic, like, ever. I've got years of experience dealing with violence, and I just don't lose my cool when the shit hits the fan. I'm the kind of dude you want making decisions in dangerous situations. Enough about me, I'm writing history now. More about me later when I have less to write about.

I knew she was dead. Or at least, damn close to it. None of the channels would work so I grabbed my laptop and fired it up. After connecting to my network I went to all the news websites and immediately found out I was right. Picture after picture after cell phone video after news broadcast. All showing the zombies. Of course, no one had the fucking balls to call it like that. People were calling it everything but. Theories abounded everywhere I pointed the mouse. But I knew. You could see it. They were dead already, and didn't attack others until they'd passed on. I knew I needed to know a few things immediately about whatever it was that was doing this, so I got all scientific, and went to the CDC website.

They were on the ball, thankfully, and had the info as best as they could, already up. I needed to know a few things specifically:

- Transmission. How did it get transmitted? According to the CDC transmission occurred only via bite. Scratches did not seem to pass along the sickness/curse/virus/evil. Further, they had confirmed that the illness did not spread to non-human victims. Apparently a farm in Pennsylvania had all their cows eaten by the zombies and they stayed dead. (Of course later on I realized that this was somewhat wrong. You see by that point I don't think they had realized that anyone who died and didn't get their nugget wrecked immediately would get back up, seeking out flesh, being a general motherfucking nuisance to the living. But, I worked with what I knew at that point)

- Did they eat flesh? The CDC confirmed that yes, they did indeed eat the flesh of the living.

- Were the undead/sick/ill/terrorists that ate flesh more or less dangerous than a normal human being? Once again the CDC reported that the ill were slow, had diminished capacity for thought and reason, and were hostile to other human beings as well as animals. They were uncoordinated, couldn't move much faster than a clumsy trot at best, and showed no ability to communicate, or to make plans of any sort.

- Where did it all start? How close was I to "ground zero?" The CDC had no fucking clue. They said that there were about ten dozen simultaneous reports from all over the world. Plus or minus a few hours, which globally speaking is pretty fucking simultaneous. As best as I could figure, I was about a two hour drive from the closest outbreaks on the eastern seaboard.

* Could they be killed, and if so, how were they killed? According to the CDC (by now my most trusted source for news regarding the current and ongoing Zombie apocalypse) any significant damage done to the brain would drop them again. So Romero, dude you were totally spot-on. Fucking A brother.

So there it was. Despite the fact that even the CDC avoided calling it a "zombie outbreak" or the "apocalypse" I fucking knew. Well, at the very least, I wasn't about to risk it. I grabbed up my phone and tried to make a few more phone calls, but no joy. All circuits still busy. So, I formulated my plan.

Mom lived about a mile away, right near downtown, right near the schools, and I knew I would swing by her place to see if she was okay. I had a few friends who lived right around town too, and I wanted to check on them. More importantly though, was a long term survival plan. My condo was shitty in terms of a place to hole up, so I needed a place to go. I knew almost immediately I would come here, back to the school. It had everything.

I would get guns, some supplies, food, and then head to the school. Ride it out from there and see what happens. As you can tell, I made it here in one piece. But that doesn't tell the whole story. Unfortunately my guilt over wasting this gas has finally reached its boiling point. Plus I'm getting really fucking tired and I need to lock the upstairs down so I can sleep soundly.

I think for my next entry I'll talk about the trip to get here. And what I found when I did.

Until next time Mr. Journal.

-Adrian

To read more about the life of Adrian Ring as he faces the Zombiepocalypse, go to: http://adriansundeaddiary.com/

Grab Your Go Bag
(...and get it right!)
By Neil Brown, Jr.

Zombie Survival Crew™ First Lieutenant Neil Brown Jr. has got the survival gig down pat. You may know him for his on-screen characters' fights with zombies or aliens in productions like *The Walking Dead* and *Battle: Los Angeles*, but this wise-crackin' vato has got skills – and the Katana to back 'em up. This son of a marine takes a look at what we should all have pre-packed in our go bags for the kind of day we hope never comes.

☠ ☠ ☠ ☠ ☠

Dad always used to say "police your brass" and "you need to know whether you're hurt or injured." And that's just the way he raised me—to live a clean life, depend on common sense and preparation to get me through life's bumps and bruises, and develop the mental fortitude to push through the hurts.

Served me well even from a young age. When I was about 12, on one of our many family salt water fishing trips, I tumbled off the side of the boat in the early morning while everyone else was still sleeping. I know, I know. Shouldn't have been hanging over the side of the boat in the first place.

Even though I was terrified and screaming like crazy, I remembered what my dad taught me—tie the ends of my pants together, lift the whole thing up over the water and push down to grab the air and make a mini-life preserver. It worked. I bobbed in the water for several minutes before my dad dove in to rescue me. And it was about ten years before my dad or I told mom about the incident. What? She never would have let me go on another fishing trip.

It was common sense and preparation that saved me all those years ago, and that very same combination is our best shot during a cataclysmic event, like a Zombiepocalypse.

As for me, I can catch a rabbit, squirrel or fish in the woods faster than I can find you a gas station, so my go bag is naturally geared more towards hunting and gathering—even so it's a combination of items that will serve any would-be survivor well.

1 – Weapon – Some people, a-hem, may have a 9mm at home. If ya got it, pack it! Otherwise, take a look around your house at what you can improvise. Everyone's got a bat or a stick lying around. Pound some nails into it, wrap some duct tape around to secure and you've got a pretty good weapon. You want something that will give you an extension to your arm, to your natural reach.

2 – Toilet Paper – And not just for the obvious reason. Toilet paper can be used for many purposes in a survival situation. When toilet paper production stops, a whole lotta people gonna be in a lot of shit. A few rolls? Gonna be worth their weight in gold to some people (see number 8).

3 - Sustenance – Military-style MREs are a great food source and you can pick them up at a survival store. If not, grab some beef jerky, granola and dried foods like fruit or those that require nothing more than a little water, such as powdered soups, at your local grocery.

4 - First Aid Kit – This is an item you absolutely do not want to be without. You can pick up a standard version at any number of stores, but consider personalizing it. Mine's gonna have a wrap or two in it, for my knee and any sprains I might pick up runnin'.

5 – Fluids –Seems almost silly to say it, but you need water. Given that natural water sources might become infected, this could be an issue, so something to collect rainwater in—a bottle or canteen. Purification tablets are a good idea as well.

6 – Hunting Knife –You've got to have a strong blade if you have nothing else. A man and a knife can always get by…and a blade doesn't need ammo to keep functioning. A whetstone to keep the knife company is a solid item to have as well.

7 – Shoes & Socks – You're gonna be spending a lot of time on your feet so make sure you will be able to take care of them. You have got to keep your feet dry, so an extra couple pairs of socks is vital. Pack a good pair of comfortable walking shoes, boots or sneakers.

8 – Commodities – Gold, silver, cigarettes, coffee, small but valuable items you could trade for a can of gasoline. You never know, these items could be the things to save you r life.

9 – Personal Item –Take a piece of home with you. A little something to remind you what's worth fighting for. For me? A family photo album.

Bitten

by Austin Wulf

Bitten follows the final moments in the life of a woman, Emily, after she is bitten by a zombie. Her husband, Zach, pulls her into an alley, attempting to hide from the horde of zombies out on the street. While Emily deals with the emotions involved with her imminent death, Zach tries to protect her from the zombies her cries attract. When Zach realizes Emily's bite is infected, he does his best to comfort her as she falls slowly from human to zombie.

About the author:

Austin Wulf is a Colorado-based freelance writer with a rough style that features a healthy dose of snark. In his spare time he makes music and drinks good bourbon. He's well prepared for the zombie apocalypse after writing his way through it with "Dead Men Walking", a fiction blog about a lone survivor. Visit Austin on the web at www.austinwulf.com

Twitter handle: @AustinWulf

Weapon of choice: sawed-off shotgun

Bitten

We ran. Tired feet slammed against asphalt. Chests rose and fell in short bursts of breath. My heart felt ready to burst. Out of nowhere, I was struck by pain and collapsed in the street. Legs rushed past my head; the others kept on without me.

"Emily!" Zach's voice. He crouched next to me, also out of breath. "Don't worry," he said. "I have you."

All I saw was sky as he pulled me out of the street. A crowd of those—things—rushed by after our group. Their groan, that terrible sound of a thousand starved stomachs, filled my ears. The ground was cold and rough under me, and then wet. Zach propped me up against something that stank like the monsters that were chasing us.

"Gross," I said. I looked up at Zach.

"Sorry," he said, and brushed a few stray hairs from my face. "You're safe now."

I watched the shine of Zach's ring as he touched my face and thought of our wedding day. It was wonderful. In that alley, though, behind a dumpster, being chased by those creatures – and on top of it all, a cold, wet, smelly ass—being at the altar with Zach seemed like a long time ago. I listened for signs of the creatures chasing us. The echo of their moans had faded from the alley, but I still smelled them. Then again, I probably just smelled the dumpster.

Zach examined my shoulder.

"What's up?" I asked.

"Your shoulder," he said. "Did you get bit?"

"What?" I felt where he'd been inspecting; it stung. I winced a bit. "It's nothing," I said. "Probably just a scratch from when I fell."

"Look at your hand," Zach said.

Blood stained the tips of my fingers.

"You got bit," he said. "Your shirt's ripped there." He pointed to my sleeve. "Shit," he said, "there's teeth marks."

"It's fine," I said. "Come on, we've got to catch up with the others." I tried to get up, but Zach held me back. He ripped my sleeve and pulled it down.

"They'll be okay. You won't. Relax, Emily."

"What do you mean I won't?"

He stood and pulled his own shirt off. "I'm gonna try to clean it," he said. He leaned over and dabbed my shoulder.

"Ouch! That stings," I said.

"I'm sorry. It happens."

"Just stop it, okay? I told you it's nothing."

"I won't." He leaned back down. A tired groan echoed into the alley.

"What was that?" I asked. I tried to look around but couldn't see past the dumpster.

"I thought they were all in that group," Zach said to himself, looking out to the street.

"What are you talking about?"

Zach got up. "Stay there," he said to me. He walked around the dumpster, out of my view. His footsteps echoed softly under the low wail of a lost soul. That terrible sound—like the cries of a hungry child, but different somehow, lifeless—filled the alley.

I shuddered.

"Get back," Zach's voice called.

I closed my eyes tight and curled into myself. The *boom* of a gun shot echoed over the groan and I heard a *splat*. I kept my eyes closed as footsteps came back towards me.

"Emily?" Zach faded into view with blood spattered on his chest and face.

"Zach," I said, "are you okay?"

"I'm fine. I had to protect you," he said. He knelt down. "Are you?"

"That's disgusting," I said, focused on the blood.

He wiped my face with his dirty shirt.

"Get off," I said, pushing him. "I can't believe you got that shit on me." I tried to stand, but fell back down. Dirty water splashed up my back and I sobbed. "I can't take this anymore. Get me out of here!"

"Emily, you're gonna get infected." Zach held me against the wall and started dabbing at my shoulder again. "Oh, shit," he said.

"What?" I felt my wound. Warm blood covered my fingers. "Can't you clean it?"

"No." His face dropped.

"What is it?"

"It's—" He sat and put his arm around me. "It's...too late." He sighed, defeated.

"What do you mean? Stuff that thing in there," I said. "Stop the bleeding."

Zach shook his head. "It's starting to swell up, and the skin around it is red. It's infected, Emily. *You're* infected."

"I'm not infected," I said. "I can't be. Take care of me, Zach."

"I am taking care of you," he said. "Or, I'm trying."

"Can't you do anything?"

"There's nothing."

"Then at least save yourself," I said.

"I won't leave you." He touched my face softly. "I just can't." Tears fell over his cheek.

"No, don't," I said, dabbing them. "Maybe there's something we can do. Take me to a hospital."

"A hospital?"

"Sure. They can take care of me. They can clean this. Not like we can in this dirty alley. Right?"

"Emily," he said. "There *are* no hospitals. The city's overrun with those zombie things."

"There has to be something," I pleaded. "Carry me somewhere cleaner. Please?"

"I don't think so, love. I hate to be pessimistic, but I don't think you'd make it to a hospital. Even if we could find one."

"This isn't how it's supposed to happen," I said through tears. "How can you let me die like this?" '

"I wish there were something I could do," he said.

"It's disgusting." I cried harder, grabbing my shoulder. "I don't want to do this."

"Love, I think there's more coming." Zach looked impatient.

"You can't just stand there and let this *thing*—" I stopped short. "Zach?"

"Yes?"

I reached out. I heard his voice, but I couldn't see him. In my babbling I hadn't noticed my vision fade.

"Emily?"

"Zach," I said. "Where are you?"

"I'm here," I heard him say. "I'm not going anywhere."

The screeching of the undead echoed through the alley again, drowning out Zach's voice. Another group was coming through, and it was close. I didn't want that to be the last sound I heard.

"I love you, Zach." I felt his hand on my face, warm.

"I love you, too."

"I don't want to be without you," I said.

"You won't be for long."

His hand stayed with me even though I couldn't see him. The alley filled with noise and I knew it was all over. That groan, the horrible noise of death, surrounded everything.

Soon the sound faded, too. All that was left was the grimy water beneath me and the smell of rotting death and trash. I didn't want to die like that, in a disgusting alley. Then a warm hand touched my shoulder, and the pain faded.

In the last instant I felt an insatiable hunger, like I hadn't eaten in years. Everything went white, like static between TV channels. All my senses faded except for smell.

And the hunger. Oh, the hunger.

Zombies & Religion: Voodoo
by RC Murphy

ZSC Orange Brigade Commander RC Murphy takes a look at real world zombies created through religious ritual. Zombies manufactured in this manner differ from the Romero-esque fiends looking for a brain banquet. Like other zombies we know to already exist around us, these walkers may require a different engagement strategy.

☠   ☠   ☠   ☠   ☠

You're walking down the street on the way to work, same path you take every day. Up ahead a stranger steps out of a shop and walks your direction. Even though you try to move out of the way, they bump into you. After a few muttered apologies, they walk on. Only then do you notice that your forearm is numb and bleeding from a small cut. Within minutes that entire side of your body loses sensation. A little while later you are unable to control any of your body's movements.

You've been turned into a zombie.

How can it be that easy, you ask? If you lived in Haiti, where Voodoo reigns supreme, there would be no question about the existence of zombies. However, unlike other "breeds" of undead, zombies created by Voodoo are living, breathing humans.

Zombie victims are dosed with a neurotoxin. There has been extensive debate about which neurotoxin is used during the zombie making process. In the film *The Serpent and the Rainbow*, victims were given a dose of tetrodotoxin powder. Tetrodotoxin can be found in puffer fish and its history of being extremely lethal in small doses puts the legitimacy of these claims into question. But for the sake of simplicity, we'll use it here.

Tetrodotoxin works on the nervous system, effectively shutting it down. The victim's breathing will become shallow. Their body is completely unresponsive to stimulation. While they cannot feel, move, or breathe properly, most victims remain fully aware of what is happening to them in this state of living death.

Treatment of tetrodotoxin poisoning involves maintaining the body's functions until it processes the chemical. Most villages don't have the means to put someone on life support, let alone the manpower and supplies to put someone on life support that may pass away with or without medical intervention. Tetrodotoxin has no known antidote. Once the physician sees no visible signs of life, they declare the patient deceased. The victim then ends up being buried alive.

In the cover of darkness a Bokor, the sorcerer that ordered the zombie to be made, will venture to the graveyard to dig up the victim. At this time the newly made zombie is given a powerful hallucinogenic. Most believe the substance to be derived from the datura plant. Datura causes violent hallucinations and photophobia (extreme sensitivity to light). One dose will affect the victim for approximately 48 hours.

The heavy influence of the Voodoo religion in the country is the key element to the zombie creation process. If the victim survives exposure to the various chemical compounds at play, they should recover themselves within days. Believers that go through the process convince themselves, with influence from the Bokor, that they are in fact a reanimated corpse. These zombies will continue to work under the bokor for years believing this. It is only when family members see them that legitimacy of their "undead" condition comes into question.

Bokors are believed to be able to manipulate the zombie astral, the spirit of a person. What we call the soul. Those that practice dark arts (making zombies, curses, etc...) capture souls inside jars. Some will sell the jars as charms. Others collect them. The more captured souls in their control, the more powerful the bokor. To go against a powerful bokor is begging to be "cursed" or have your soul captured. A dark sorcerer will go to great lengths to punish those who oppose them. That is why so many of these living zombies strive to believe their undead condition and remain in service to the bokor.

If the family recovers their loved one, they won't find much of that person left. Years of believing yourself dead and exposure to powerful hallucinogenic drugs warps the brain. Zombies without a bokor riding herd on them often end up in asylums. Those who aren't discovered tend to haunt graveyards, as they feel closer to the dead than the living.

The Zombie Survival Crew™ considers these zombies to be victims. That is, unless they attempt to harm a crewmember. Unfortunately it is difficult to tell them apart from the other breeds. Keep in mind that newly claimed zombies of this type would appear sweaty. Their eye movements erratic, and though it will be difficult to tell, they are breathing. If you think you have found a victim of a Voodoo spell, report the zombie but do not dispatch them. Command will take care of the zombie as needed.

Zombie Girl

by Tasmin Bowerman

Sadie is a normal girl living with her mother, well, as normal as a girl who collects zombies can be. She didn't start out to collect zombies, it just sort of happened...starting with the zombie animals who sought her out, and then Jess, the little girl. Predictably, the neighbors do not understand why Sadie feels the need to take care of the zombies and, as with most things not understood, fear develops.

About the author:

As a child, Tasmin's imaginary friends hung out in mirrors. Now they tell her stories which she writes down when she can. She lives in the middle of nowhere with zombie bunnies (but don't tell anyone) and too many books. Her weapon of choice is a rifle with enough ammo to supply a small army, a katana as backup, and, if worst comes to worst, her strategy is to hide behind ZSC Red Brigade Commander Juliette's crossbow. You can find Tasmin on twitter as @Lainasparetime.

Zombie Girl

It started with pets. I woke one morning to a familiar scratching noise and found my dog on my front porch.

The dog who died a month ago.

Barney didn't hurt anyone and he didn't eat much, so we let him stay. Mom worried at first he might start dropping hunks of fur – or flesh – on the floor, but if possible, he shed less in undeath than he did in life.

Barney was the first, but he wasn't the last. We hadn't buried any other pets, but our neighbours had. When the owners turned their deceased pets away, the animals ended up on my doorstep. I couldn't bring myself to make them leave, but letting them in the house wasn't an option. Mom put up with Barney. The other animals? Not so much.

She did, however, let me keep our old shed open for them. I put food out sometimes, but they never ate it. Neither did any living animals. In fact, fewer live creatures came around our house every day. Mom and I didn't mind much. The raccoons finally stopped getting into our garbage.

The neighbours whispered about me when the fourth silent dog slipped into the shed. The whispers increased when two birds and a rabbit joined the other animals. They neared shouts when the horse showed up, but where else could he go?

Eventually, I found an open-minded farm where the horse had room to run. Mostly because he kept kicking up Mom's flower beds.

It hurt a little when people started calling me "Zombie Girl," but I ignored them. And after a while, they lost interest. A few dead animals, even ones still walking around, weren't as interesting as the latest celebrity gossip.

Until the girl appeared on our front step.

She freaked me out. Seeing as I slept with a dead dog on the end of my bed, that said a lot. Not that there was anything wrong with her, per se. She had all her parts, no bits of skin dropping off or loose teeth. Even her light blonde hair stayed long and thick. Dull, not anything like the shiny hair children her age usually possessed, but long and thick nonetheless.

But when I opened the door and those flat silver eyes stared at me, I shrieked and slammed the door shut. Five minutes later, when I worked up the courage to open the door, she hadn't moved so much as an inch.

Mom wasn't happy about the girl. But Jess wouldn't tell me anything about her parents. I couldn't contact them about her. Like my animals, she had nowhere to go and I became responsible for her survival, much like I was for the animals. I mean, she couldn't have been more than nine when she died. Where else could she go?

Jess didn't talk much. She sat for hours staring at the TV, unmoving and barely blinking. The light flickering in her empty eyes gave me the heebie-jeebies. I often left her there alone.

Barney liked the television, too. He never barked, but he grew extra quiet when I turned the set in my room on. He let me pet him again then. I missed petting him while he was… gone. After he came back, he wouldn't let me touch him, except when the TV was on.

We watched a lot of movies.

Things quieted down again. If the neighbours whispered about me, I didn't hear it. I knew Jess made people uneasy, but she stayed hidden in the house and no one complained about her. At least, not to our faces.

My animal count stayed the same for a few weeks. Maybe they sensed I didn't have room for them yet. In the lull, I cleaned off the shelves in the shed for the birds, tore up old blankets for nesting supplies, and dug some of my old clothes out of the attic. Jess needed things that actually fit.

When Logan showed up, the neighbours freaked. Like Jess, there was nothing wrong with him. Quite the opposite, in fact. He spoke with an ease none of the others exhibited. He didn't walk with the stumbling gait the majority of the living dead shared. If it weren't for his flat silver eyes, you wouldn't be able to tell.

But he brought so many other zombies with him. Children, not adults. Young kids, some who couldn't have been more than five, but none older than ten or eleven. Stuffed toys, security blankets and all.

It took a while for him to open up to me. When he did, I learned he and his little brother died in a car crash several hundred miles away. Their parents refused to take them in after they woke up. They came here for reasons I didn't understand, children joining them as they travelled.

Seven children, plus Logan's brother, and Jess. Nine undead children total.

Mom and I didn't know what to do or where to put them. I never saw Jess or the others sleep. When you look at children, though, you think they need beds. It's only natural. Luckily, we had an empty basement and sleeping bags. They seemed most comfortable there, anyways. Maybe—actually, I didn't want to think about that one.

At first, my mother didn't want them in the house. Who would, honestly? But I asked her to imagine if I were the one in their shoes. She agreed they needed us. Children, even zombie children, can't survive alone.

The neighbours talked when Mom and I let the kids stay, talked louder when I took them to the mall to buy clothes. But most of the new arrivals came with ragged, dirty clothes barely holding together. They needed new things.

The voices got louder still when I wanted to take the kids to the park.

Logan argued with the idea, like he did whenever I planned outings, but I told him dead or not, children needed to play. I thought spending a couple hours outside in the sun and warmth might help them remember how they used to be.

There was a particular way the undead stared. A blank, flat gaze from those coin-coloured eyes. I imagined it unnerved most people. Logan tried it on me, like that would make me agree with him. He must have forgotten how much time I spent with my dead animals.

Maybe I convinced him. Maybe he grew sick of my pestering.

Logan and I decided to take just three of the kids, thinking a small group would be best. His brother, Jess, and a little girl with faded copper hair who I could draw aboveground if I promised she could play with the rabbits. When I told the kids what I planned, they turned the same blank silver gazes on me, but didn't ask questions. They trusted me.

The way people at the park reacted, you would have thought we brought an entire army of undead children. They chased us home.

The kids refused to go out for weeks, even into the backyard. I let them hide inside for a while, but after the second week, I was fed up.

I asked Logan to go out for coffee with me to talk. He looked at me funny for a minute, his dark eyebrows drawing together in a frown. I didn't realize why until the coffee he'd ordered turned cool on the table. I'd forgotten he didn't eat or drink. With Logan, it was easy to forget.

When we got home, I pinned him against the door and kissed him until my head spun. I worried about what he would taste like, but all I tasted was mint. After a few seconds, I stopped worrying entirely.

Someone saw us. The neighbours hated it. They called me names. To my face, behind my back, to the media that camped out on the front lawn hoping to get a shot of us kissing. Living girls didn't kiss dead boys. I was a novelty, a freak, and everyone knew my name. Everyone knew Sadie, the Zombie Girl.

The kids hid in the basement.

I yelled about the cameras a lot, because I couldn't yell at the reporters. It would look bad. Only in the house, but didn't matter in the end. A camera taped me through a window and the silent footage played everywhere. The world watched me ranting, pacing back and forth like a lunatic, and the whole world saw Logan kiss me.

They played that part more than the rest. It was the first time his face was made public. The newspapers splashed it next to mine and they targeted him like they targeted me. Frankenstein, worm food, every name they called him broke my heart.

I received enough hate mail to fill an Olympic swimming pool. My email address got posted on some website and I had to delete it. We changed our phone number three times, and none of the kids left the house. Jess hid in the basement with the others, not even tempted by the television now.

Logan stopped kissing me, which sucked. He stopped talking to me about anything important and retreated downstairs with the kids, leaving just me and Mom upstairs. It made me lonely in a way I never expected. I started this thing out alone. I should have been used to it.

Then someone threw a rock through our living room window while Mom was at work. I broke down and sobbed, certain we were all doomed because of me and my actions, while Logan boarded up the window. When I stopped crying, he hugged me. He didn't say a word, but his embrace spoke louder than any words.

We curled up on the couch and turned on a movie. One by one, the kids drifted up from the basement, sitting in neat lines on the floor in front of the couch. A little strange, perhaps, but what could you expect? Maybe after being dead, the order comforted them. Or something like that.

Orange light flickering through the boards interrupted the movie. My stomach sank and my spine went cold. Whatever it was, I knew it wasn't good. When we heard the shouts, half the kids took off for the basement. The other half ran towards the windows. I told Logan to get them into the basement, too, and headed for the front door. Of all the things people had done, this was the worst. No one—no one—got to invade my home like this.

The people lighting my front lawn on fire called me a necrophile, among other things. My fists balled at my sides and my face scorched from the heat of the fire, I shouted a few choice names at the top of my lungs. Monsters, lunatics, everything I could think of while my lawn burned.

It would have ended there, except small, cold fingers clutched at my arms. Someone shouted and I dragged Jess behind me. No matter what anybody thought, she was a kid and needed to be protected.

The noise sounded like thunder magnified. I managed Jess' name once before the fire in my chest made it impossible to speak. Then everything went black. For a long time, I floated alone in the darkness.

Logan was there when I woke, though he shouldn't have been. He snuck into the morgue with clothes, somehow knowing I'd need them, and took me home.

Waking up naked on a slab was not an experience I ever cared to repeat. My mother's face when her dead daughter walked through the front door was not a sight I ever wanted to see again. But when Jess pounced on me, wrapped her thin arms around my waist, it made the other things easier. Not easy. But easier.

The kids still spend too much time in the basement. I understand it now, but Mom hates when I drift down there. Part of her doesn't want to admit what I am. Part of me doesn't, either. Part of me hates that I crave the cool, damp darkness of the basement. I pretend to sleep in my bedroom at night so Mom and I can pretend I'm human.

It doesn't always work.

Mom cancelled our cable when the news started playing the video nightly. She cried every time they showed the shooting, and it made the kids and Logan too quiet. It wasn't an easy thing for them to process. Logan hid his anger in his silence. In their own way, the kids hid their grief that I am no longer human.

As for me... I left the room when it was on.

Now we watch more movies than ever.

The animals keep coming. Ever since I died, they don't allow anyone living onto our property unless I tell them to. Besides my mother, of course. Most people don't try now. The breathers, as the kids call them, still hate my undead animals. Even the bunnies unnerve them.

For the most part, I try to ignore the news. We're living, surviving, and that's what matters. But sometimes I go online when Mom's asleep and the kids are watching movies upstairs. When it's just Logan and me in the basement with my laptop. My morbid curiosity gets the best of me.

Some days I find things that give me hope. Hope that people will learn to accept and understand them—us. Stories of people following my example and giving homes to undead children or animals. But some days the things I find only make me cry. I appreciate Logan all the more on those days.

I'm always grateful for him. Sometimes I find it harder to talk now, my tongue thick and awkward in my mouth and the words twisting in my head. He's as patient with me as I've seen him be with the kids. I understand now why they followed him. What I don't understand is why they came to me, why the animals keep coming... but Logan says I will. Someday. I'm willing to wait for those answers.

They still call me Zombie Girl.

But I Do Love You For Your Brain
(A Zombie Love Story)
by Jessica Capelle

Erik and Jaimy have a relationship that's filled with love and commitment. There's just one problem… she wants to eat him. He works hard to keep her grounded in the world of the living, but Amanda, Jaimy's best friend, wants her to embrace all aspects of being undead, including munching on Erik, buffet-style. Erik knows that he's fighting an impossible battle, but he's become a zombie in many ways himself. When he's left vulnerable, will Jaimy's love save him or will she embrace her true nature and destroy him?

About the author:

Jessica Capelle keeps busy with everything from corporate law to tutoring to tech support when she's not writing. She's currently seeking representation for her first novel, a YA paranormal romance. You can find out more about Jessica at www.jessicacapelle.com or on Twitter @jessicacapelle.

Weapon of choice: Machete

But I Do Love You For Your Brain
(A Zombie Love Story)

"I have to put my foot down, Jaimy. I mean it."

"Mmmmm… foot. Jaimy like foot."

She grins, and her jaw sags. It makes her look like the Joker. Good thing I like Batman.

"Focus, sweetie. I'm serious. Amanda can't come over if she's going to attack me. Don't you understand how that makes me feel?"

"But foot good. Jaimy hungry."

"Enough with the foot!" I yell.

Jaimy's bottom lip drops below her chin, the zombie version of a pout.

"I'm sorry, honey," I sigh. "Let's just finish the movie, okay?"

She snuggles up to me and digs her head into my neck. The familiar smell of mold mixed with coconut shampoo clings to her limp, matted hair. No matter how often she showers, the mildew smell lingers. I've come to love that smell.

I never planned to have a member of the undead as my girlfriend. My opinion of zombies had always been they were disgusting, unnatural creatures. Hell, they only existed in bad horror films until two years ago. No one's sure how it started, but the current ratio of undead to "stays dead" is about even.

After the initial panic, the government held mandatory classes on how to deal with zombies. Unlike the film versions, our zombies behaved pretty much like when they were alive. Once you got past their steep decline in I.Q. and their cravings for human flesh, you could almost forget what they were. Congress fast-tracked legislation to make it a crime to kill a zombie unless you were under attack.

Zombie rights groups formed soon after, and the push for integration led to hate-crime legislation. The compromise was the installation of "big brother" cameras on every corner. With the cameras, you could prove you only acted to save yourself. Zombie hate crimes are pretty rare now, although I suspect that's because many people provoke zombies into coming after them.

Jaimy will graduate from King High this year, unless there's another unfortunate incident with a teacher. But it's really not her fault. Amanda is to blame for Jaimy's slip-ups. She always tries to get Jaimy to eat people and destroy things. Just because they're zombies doesn't mean they can't be civilized, but Amanda has completely embraced her inner zombie.

Like most afternoons, we're watching a Lifetime movie, Jaimy's favorite. Since they keep her calm, I don't mind. Too much. I put my arm around her torso to adjust her so her bony elbow isn't impaling my side anymore.

Crunch.

I gasp, knowing I've just shattered another rib. Jaimy still has that "Joker grin" plastered across her distorted face, so I'm guessing she didn't feel a thing.

"I'm so sorry, baby! Are you okay?"

"Jaimy okay. Love Erik."

She looks up at me, and I melt right into the couch, broken rib forgotten. Dead or not, those eyes still get to me. Jaimy has a profound effect on men, and death hasn't diminished it. A few weeks ago, she so completely mesmerized this guy at the bus stop that it took him a minute to realize that she was gnawing on his hand. I shiver at the memory of what happened to him after that. If I ever let my guard down for one minute, I would likely have the same fate.

"Erik cold? Jaimy warm up."

Her hands hold my face in a vise-like grip as she pulls me toward her deformed lips. Zombies are surprisingly strong for dead people. After a long, drool-soaked kiss, she pushes me back and feels around in her mouth. She opens it unnaturally wide as she yanks a loose tooth out of her decaying gums, and a smell similar to rancid meat fills my nose for just a second. As the acid rises in my throat, she giggles and mumbles something about the Tooth Fairy. It doesn't take me long to compose myself since I'm used to it by now. Dating a zombie, you learn quickly that you have to watch out for errant body parts.

Jaimy starts to kiss and gnaw on my ear. When she first became a zombie and would do this, I had nightmares about giant rats every night. Sometimes I'd wake up to her tenderizing my toes. After a "situation" left her brother without a hand, I took my key back. I think her parents lock her in her room at night now. But truth be told, plenty of living girls I dated before Jaimy committed worse make-out atrocities, like too much tongue or breathing too hard in my ear. Teething is just Jaimy's make-out "quirk".

I have to pay attention though; she's already taken a chunk out of my neck twice. But injuries are a small price to pay to keep the girl I love. I can't imagine being with anyone else, and we still plan to get married soon. We'll have to adopt of course, and I'll hire a bodyguard for the baby.

Jaimy moans in a way I know isn't sexual, so I pull her off my neck. The little bites that run from my left ear to my shoulder burn. She foams at the mouth and pants like a rabid dog as her teeth gnash together. But despite the cannibalistic frenzy, she looks like an angel to me.

I know if I hold her off for a bit the desire to eat my flesh will leave. It takes a few minutes, but her eyes finally return to the dull, deep green of my dreams. She flashes her crooked smile at me, and I push her chin back into place.

"Did you get a dress today?"

"Black. Lace. Store lady not like Jaimy."

"I'm sure she liked you. You're perfect."

"Jaimy bit lady."

She looks down and cringes, expecting me to yell. I take in a couple of deep breaths to keep my voice calm.

"You can't bite people, honey. We talked about this."

"Not mean to. So hungry. Jaimy sorry. Erik no love Jaimy?"

Tears drip through the gash under her right eye as she looks up at me. She begins to tentatively smile, though, as I stroke her face and touch the center of her cold lips. The worst thing in the world to me is to see my precious girl upset. When I found out she was a zombie, I told her I couldn't see her anymore. Her reaction nearly killed me. I could see it all over her pasty, grey face; if I left her, the Jaimy I knew would be lost, consumed by zombie nature. From that moment, I knew I'd do whatever it took to keep her from becoming a monster.

We sit silently for several minutes, my heartbeat like drums compared to her soft thump. Scientists think zombie hearts function only enough for basic movement and speech, which is why they're so clumsy and awkward and speak like toddlers. Jaimy isn't the same as she was when I met her, but she's still my girl. I just don't know for how long.

Suddenly the door flies open, shattering our quiet moment. A horrific smell of stale blood, rotten gore, and manure hits me. Amanda.

"Were you born in a barn, Amanda?"

"Tell more joke, loser. I hurt you."

She glares at me.

"Jaimy, come. Food time."

I grab Jaimy's hand to stop her, but she's already up. Amanda laughs and points at me. Jaimy is a few steps away when she turns, her detached hand still in mine.

"Erik fix Jaimy after food," she says between giggles.

"Jaimy, please don't kill anyone. Go to the hospital and get someone who just died. No fresh people, okay?"

The pout returns to her face.

"But Jaimy like life. Jaimy like warm."

I shake my head and throw up my hands. Jaimy's quick to appease me.

"Okay Erik. No warm."

Her body language tells me she's lying, but at least she'll feel guilty about it when she comes home.

"Come Jaimy. Do what daddy say," Amanda snarls.

I really hate that zombie.

They barely lift their feet as they walk across the tile and out the front door: the Zombie Shuffle. They'll kill someone, brutally I'm sure, but what can I do? I've tried to get Jaimy to eat animals, like one of those vegetarian vampires, or to at least eat only already dead or dying people. But the zombie cravings are strong. It's harder for her to fight them off now, and I know I'll lose her completely before long. I can't think about it too much, because I can never go back either. I'm as much of a zombie as Jaimy now.

My life revolved around Jaimy when she was alive, and it isn't any different now. I must have a death wish to stay with so deadly a creature, right? But she doesn't feel dangerous to me. She's just Jaimy, and she needs my protection. Even in this dark world, Jaimy is my light, which is ironic since I'm the one who killed her.

A deer ran in front of the truck. If I'd seen it, I could've swerved. The police ruled it an accident; death by deer happens all the time in the country. But I know the truth. I killed her. I drove too fast and didn't pay attention to the road. Being with undead Jaimy is my penance: my own little heaven and hell, all rolled into one.

Amanda's evil laugh drifts up the sidewalk. Feeding time must be over. I turn toward the sound as the pieces of the door explode into the room, and a large chunk flies straight at me. Amanda lowers her twisted right leg, the one that just kicked the door in, and pops it back into place with a horrible crunch. It's ridiculous how strong zombies can be, especially considering how easily they come apart.

An evil grin spreads across her face as she shuffles toward me through the wreckage. She licks her lips and prowls around the living room: a lioness stalking her prey. Jaimy hasn't come in yet, but I'm not sure she'd help me anyway.

I reach up and feel the blood trickle out of the deep gash in my forehead. No wonder Amanda eyes me like we're on a nature program. She moves forward slowly, and I slide sideways, my hands searching for a weapon behind me.

"Yummy Erik. 'Manda taste you now."

"I don't think so nasty girl. I'm no zombie buffet."

Adrenaline keeps me alert despite the blood loss, and I circle back toward the fireplace. Amanda snarls and lunges at me. Just in time, I grab the fireplace poker and shove it forward into her belly as hard as I can. The impact knocks me off my feet, the back of my head connecting with the tile. She grabs at my legs and scratches at the floor as she grunts and hisses at me. One of my kicks connects with her face, and she lets go long enough for me to scramble to my knees and grab the iron shovel. I'm seeing stars but I manage to turn and bring the shovel down hard on her neck.

Ding dong, zombie gone.

The way to kill a zombie is to behead or burn her, and burning just seems cruel.

Just then I notice Jaimy. She walks around the couch toward the body, looking scared and uncertain.

"Amanda dead?"

"I'm sorry. I know she was your friend, but she tried to hurt me."

"Amanda hurt my Erik?"

She snarls and snaps her teeth together as she looks over at the body. I try to nod my head, but everything starts to spin. A moan escapes my lips as my legs turn to jelly. Somehow Jaimy catches me as I collapse. She lowers me to the floor, puts my head in her lap, and cradles me like a baby.

"Jaimy take care Erik now."

I'm so weak I can't answer. She rocks me, humming a strange song. The blackness pulls me under.

A big German Shepherd licks the cuts on my body. I hear the slurping and feel the hair tickling my arm. I must be dreaming because I could never keep a dog in the house with Jaimy around. While animals aren't her first choice, it would be like putting a cheeseburger in front of a dieter.

The licking feels strange but not unpleasant. Then the dog bites me on the arm. Hard. And again. I manage to open my eyes but wish I'd stayed in the dream. There's no dog, just Jaimy with my arm in her mouth.

Those gorgeous green eyes go wide and lock on mine as I squeak out her name. Her face is full of hunger, lust, and need. Blood pours down her chin. A slight flash of concern crosses her face, but it's gone quickly. I'm too weak to fight her off and too exhausted to be horrified by what she's done.

Her gaze softens for a moment, and she touches the side of my face. She leans forward and brushes her lips across the gash in my forehead. As she lingers there, breath cold on the cut in my scalp, I know what will happen next. It's in those eyes that I love. She won't ask permission, but she doesn't want to force me either.

I tried to be everything to her, her anchor to the living, but she'll never be tamed. My Jaimy is gone. The monster replaced her. The monster I created.

It was wrong to try to change her. I know that now. True love means letting people be who they are, and I owe her that freedom. I owe her more than I could ever repay.

As her hungry teeth go for my head, I'm confident I did the right thing in the end.

Love Me Dead or Alive

by Wendy Sparrow

Love Me Dead or Alive is the touching… nay… poignant story of Mindy who is attempting to come to grips with her own mortality as her undead boyfriend pressures her to join him so they can be together forever. Titus has more to fear than just his girlfriend's ticking mortal clock, though; an old school buddy is trying to force Titus's hand in doing a little doctoring the dead. It's the age old story of boy loves girl… girl loves boy… boy is dead and wants girl to be also but she isn't sure if she is ready for that commitment… with zombie monkeys.

About the author:

Due to the quantity of characters weighing it down, Wendy Sparrow's brain weighs 3 lbs 5 oz. It's quite the crowd; zombies, vampires, gargoyles, and, yes, even a few humans frolic amid her gray matter. Fueled by insomnia and Mountain Dew, Wendy exorcises even the most stubborn characters by writing their stories. When she isn't hovering over her laptop, she is parenting two wonderful quirky kids or giving her husband some attention in return for his unflagging support and devotion. It's a charmed life mostly…until the zombies find out the size of her brain.

As for weapons, I received a pistol grip crossbow for Christmas from the husband… but I still intend to trip and use others as bait.
Wendy can be found frolicking on twitter as @WendySparrow

Love Me Dead Or Alive

The incessant dinging of the doorbell could either mean trouble or the neighbor kids. Titus opened the door just as Mindy dropped dead at his feet. Again. She needed to stop doing this. He snatched her up off the ground and carried her into his back room, laying her on the metal table. It looked like blood loss was the culprit this time. He lifted her shirt to see two stab wounds. Holy crap. She had to take more time off. Using the searing wand, he burnt the wounds closed while covering his nose. Burnt flesh smelled bad enough, but Mindy's burnt flesh creeped him out like nothing else could.

Finally, when he was certain she wasn't just going to die all over again, he stabbed the hypodermic in her chest and flooded her heart with the solution before he hit her with the magnetic pulse.

"C'mon, Mindy," he whispered. He watched the monitors for her vital signs to spike.

Crap. He hit her again with the magnetic pulse.

The beat of her heart made him sigh. Her wounds started closing up as the enriched blood pumped through. Every time he did this he experienced a Dr. Frankenstein moment where he wanted to yell, "It's alive," but Mindy probably wouldn't appreciate it... at all. Then again, he didn't appreciate her dying on him.

Her eyes fluttered open, and she smiled at him.

"Hey, Beautiful." Titus leaned over her and brushed some hair from her eyes. "You woke up just in time. I was starting to worry I was developing necrophilia. It turns out you look hotter alive than dead."

She laughed.

"So, stop dying on me," he said.

She winced suddenly.

"What? What's wrong?" She really needed to stop the vigilante business.

"My shoulder. I think that freak I took down knocked it out of its socket," she said.

His jaw tightened with disapproval as he leaned over and felt her shoulder. She just had to stop. If not for herself... for him....

"Don't, Titus."

"Don't what, Mindy? Don't worry about you?"

"It's not that bad."

He shoved down and pulled on her arm. She screamed in pain and curled into a ball. Tucking his frame around hers, Titus rubbed the muscles on her back. She already showed signs of healing, but that hurt them both every time.

"I'm fine."

"You're not, Mindy. This is getting ridiculous. Do you know how hard it is seeing you dead? No, you don't because I don't keep dying on you."

"It doesn't KEEP happening," she said, sitting up.

"Fifth time, babe. Fifth time," he said, cleaning up the crash kit he kept near the door for just such occasions. "What if I can't get to you within eight minutes? You know how complicated it is to restore brain cells in someone with oxygenated blood and a beating heart. They don't always work right. You could end up as a real zombie." He threw the syringe in the disposal, and it shattered which actually seemed to help his mood. "Not to mention I've never done this more than nine times on anything. Chester might have had nine lives in him, but who knows if you do. You're a lot more complicated than a freaking cat, Mindy."

She wrapped her arms around him from behind. "Shh, Titus," she said. Her skin felt warm, and he tried to pretend it wasn't nice... that he didn't like the heat radiating off her. He rubbed his hands across her arms. If her skin was cold, it wouldn't matter; he'd still love her... with all his cold, silent heart.

"It took two magnetic blasts this time, Mindy." He traced circles on her arm around his waist. It was nice having her still be alive, but it also made things a lot more dangerous.

"I'll be more careful, I promise." She'd promised that before.

"Just let me do it, babe," Titus pleaded. "I can't even stand to think what would happen if you died for good." He'd stop her heart, flood her body with the new blood, and they wouldn't have to worry or rush if anything happened to her. One of the nice little perks of being undead. Nothing just quit on you ever again... as far as they knew.

"I'm not ready," Mindy said... again. "I'll cut back at work."

"You said that last time."

"Well, Armand just sent out a fresh batch of zombies today, and I'm the only one with a Lazarus Doctor on call."

"You need to get to Armand then and quit dealing with these minions of his," Titus said. "Actually, not you... Armand is a bastard and would kill you just to get to me."

She propped her chin on his shoulder. "That'd bug you, huh?"

He turned and kissed her. He needed her, warm and alive in his arms. It would be strange when she finally gave in and let him make her immortal and shut down her heart. Her lips were soft, the moist heat of her breath addictive. She said it didn't bother her that he was already an undead, but she'd never known him before either. Maybe she missed the feel of warmth, and that's why she kept holding him off. She rubbed her body against his, and her hands slid up the back of his shirt. Sweet heat. Mindy was a dream come true... and he still remembered what those dreams were like even if he never slept anymore.

Mindy went still, and he felt her grimace against his mouth.

"What?" he asked, pulling back. Did she really feel this way? Was she repulsed and had always just hidden it? Is that why she...?

"I smell like burnt flesh." Mindy glanced down at her healed stomach. "Geez. Why didn't you tell me, Titus?"

He smiled in relief. It wasn't him. "Yeah. Not my favorite smell, babe."

"I'm going to go take a shower and change." Standing on her tiptoes for a quick kiss, she said, "Thanks for bringing me back to life, honey."

"Thanks for dying close to home, sweetheart," he said dryly as she slipped from his arms to go shower.

He really needed to talk her into becoming undead. This whole dying thing was going to be the death of him.

With the hot water beating on her skin, she finally broke down and cried. Dying scared the crap out of her. What if she didn't make it back to Titus in time? What could she do, though? She didn't want to quit her job. She made good money as a bounty hunter for brain-dead zombies. Plus, she just plain liked it.

On the other hand, this whole immortality thing scared her a little more. It was permanent whereas, thus far, death had just been a bump in the road. Titus had really looked terrified when she'd first opened her eyes. If he couldn't bring her back one of these times, he'd blame himself. Even as one of the leading Lazarus Doctors, he had his limitations... and no one had gone beyond seven times with a human who hadn't undergone the immortality procedure. Only Titus's formula had gone beyond eight times with a living thing period. She kept thinking when she hit seven, she'd ask to be made undead permanently, but could she really put Titus through this another two times? Out of fear?

No, not just fear. A bunch of different things caught her short of saying the words. Her heart still fluttered every time she kissed Titus and made her feel alive. If her heart stopped, would she still feel that way? What if she felt nothing for him? He kept telling her he felt things still, but everything she felt came from her heart. Her beating heart.

Then, there was that other matter. He tried to pretend her warm body wasn't a turn-on, but she could tell, it was. What if he stopped loving her when she wasn't warm-blooded? If she made the leap to the undead for him and his interest died too, would she be able to handle it?

No. She wouldn't.

Finally, there were her dreams. She dreamt of them together every night. Things were perfect. The sky was blue. There were trees. Trees. Just like there used to be. Titus and her would run across fields and fall laughing into the grass. The grass. Giving up her mortality would be giving up on that too. She wouldn't sleep or dream. There would be no falling asleep in Titus's arms and falling into a perfect dream. She wouldn't feel the rush of blood in her veins whenever he tipped her back for a kiss just to be silly. Her skin wouldn't blush when he'd tease her.

Cold. Still. Dreamless.

Vanessa made the jump to undead, and she said over and over "I'm cold" for like the first six months—until she forgot what it was like to be warm.

After she'd toweled dry she threw her clothes into an incinerator. Her clothes stunk, and that much blood wouldn't come out. No wonder Titus had looked so freaked out. He probably was up scrubbing his front porch right now. She snuck into his room and borrowed some clothes. An over-sized sweatshirt and a pair of his boxers would have to do until she could make a run by her apartment.

After dressing, she found him in the kitchen. He was drinking one of the protein shakes he lived on, but he nodded at the fridge, saying, "I grabbed some beating heart food for you yesterday."

Yet another strike against immortality. All you ate were those freaky, clear protein shakes. She'd tried one. They tasted just like they looked— like flavorless jello. She opened his fridge to find bread and lunchmeat. Titus had been undead for so long he didn't always know what tasted good anymore. He fell back on buying her stuff for sandwiches most of the time.

"It's okay?" he asked.

"It's good." She hugged his middle on her way to get a plate. "I like sandwiches."

She could hear the smile in voice as he said, "You really should just leave some of your clothes over here."

"I thought you liked me wearing your clothes." He'd once said seeing her in his boxers nearly made his heart start beating again. Had that already changed?

Titus laughed. "Yeah, but that sweatshirt you're wearing…."

She glanced down. It was one of his medical school shirts. "Lazarus University" it said on the front. "What does the back say?" she asked.

Leaning forward, he kissed her neck and said, "Mortality is for the uninspired." He went to crash on the couch with his protein shake in his hand. She followed a moment later to see him still trying to smother a smile.

"You're goofy," she said, tucking herself beside him.

"Hey, come here." He pulled her onto his lap. "I just need you close for a bit." The smile disappeared, replaced by worry.

"I'm okay, Titus."

"I know." He wrapped his arms around her and flipped on the news. Without asking her, he also flipped on the heated couch so she wouldn't get cold against his body. It didn't bother her. He knew that right? It seemed the wrong time to say anything. She didn't want to make a big deal of the body heat thing, so she just leaned against him and ate her sandwich. No sooner had she finished eating and set her plate to the side, than she fell asleep in his arms.

He'd switched to an old movie marathon. Half-way through "I am Legend," the call blipped on the edge of his screen. Titus considered taking Mindy into another room but she'd probably wake up either way.

He tucked the blanket around her ears and answered.

"Well, hello, Armand," he said, scowling at the image in the corner of the screen. In the middle of the screen, Will Smith continued fighting monsters. It was apropos Armand should call now.

"I see your girlfriend made it through another one of my surprise gifts," Armand said. "She must have arrived around the time I saw the power draw from your machines. Dead again? Such a shame. What number is this for her? Four? Five? It must burn that she'd rather die than let you stop her heart. What does that say about what she thinks of you, I wonder?"

"Cut the crap, Armand... what do you want?"

Mindy stirred in his arms.

"The same thing I always want, Titus." Armand ran a finger down one of the scars on his face. "Payback. Revenge."

"That was your fault, not mine. You got sloppy with your core draining after experiments. Her death is on your head, not mine. You'd only asked me to push the button... not prep the table or prepare the solution." The scars on Titus's hands from the explosion should have been payback enough for the episode. Most of the scars they incurred would heal with the right application of serums, but not these. The scars on Armand's face and those on Titus's hands were grim reminders they'd keep for eternity.

"Always an explanation. Always an excuse. Like you've never made mistakes. The great Titus. Let's not forget some of your failed experiments like to bite. Tell me, has Mindy ever taken down your series four blunders? I seem to remember they were particularly heinous."

"They were already dead when I did that," Titus said. "They were too far gone to save anyway. And I don't need to justify myself to you." Besides, he could hardly regret series four because they'd led to his discovery of the exact elixir he used today... the one breaking the barrier between death and life. Something up in his lab would blow his old medical school partner's mind... if they'd still been friends.

"Come out and do your own cleanup instead of sending your girlfriend out to do it."

"Like you do?" Titus asked. "That's what you call it when you create more drones and send them out to die?"

Armand smiled. "Touché." He leaned forward in the black leather armchair he sat in and steepled his fingers. "This competition between us bores me."

Titus raised his eyebrows. Doubtful. Armand seemed to thrive on competition.

"I need something and I'm willing to make some... concessions in exchange," Armand said.

"What?"

"What do I need or what concessions will I make?"

Mindy startled awake and turned blinking to the screen. "Armand?" she asked, rubbing her eyes.

"Good evening, Mindy. I was just telling your good doctor I'll spare your life if he gives me a full batch of the series five solution with the latest diagnostics on it... delivered personally, of course; I'd rather not have a pickaxe in my spleen like one of my last minions you met."

"Titus was probably going to tell you to go to hell," Mindy said. "There... I saved him the trouble." She sat up on his lap and tucked her arms around him. "Don't, Titus," she whispered, sensing his hesitation.

"What do you plan to do with it?" Titus asked.

"You let me worry about that," Armand said.

"No," Mindy said. "No. Whatever you've got planned... just no."

Titus leaned in and whispered, "Mindy... it might be worth it. The series five is flawless. He won't be able to do anything with it... other than what it's intended for."

"When have you ever known him not to have something nasty in mind?"

Actually, Titus had known Armand, once upon a time, to be a brilliant doctor on the rise and a good friend... before the explosion set him on this new path of destruction and mayhem.

"Your answer in one hour," Armand said, hanging up abruptly.

Titus tapped a button and Will Smith disappeared from the screen too. Then, he wished he'd left it going regardless of how inappropriate it felt; the silence had teeth.

"Titus, you can't do it," Mindy said.

"If I don't, he'll keep targeting you, Mindy, and the next time he'll succeed, and I couldn't live with myself for that." He set her off his lap and stood up to pace. He needed to think and think quickly. What on earth might Armand want with series five? It was nothing more than a healing solution... even Armand would have a difficult time corrupting its use. Armand had his own solutions he could use to reanimate corpses, but the series five wasn't like that. You couldn't use it on corpses with deep tissue damage from being in the ground. It was simple... and for healing.

"What if I agree?" Mindy whispered.

"Agree with Armand?" he asked, still pacing. It wasn't like her to change her position on anything. Mindy was stubborn.

"No, if I let you stop my heart... will you ignore this stupid trade-off with Armand?" Mindy asked.

He stopped pacing. Damn.

Titus stared at her. He seemed at a loss for words. She couldn't believe she'd said it either. After all this dancing away from the subject, would she really go through with it? Could she? She would if he took her up on the offer. He mattered more than these stupid hesitations of hers.

His mouth dropped open as he prepared to say something and then Titus just groaned and resumed pacing. He ran both his hands through his hair and groaned again. "I can't think under this much pressure," he said and strode from the room and up nearby stairs toward his regeneration/reanimation lab. She gave him a few minutes before she followed.

Titus's home was a scientist's home, clinical and cold and decorated in things easy enough to sterilize. His lab was just the opposite. Large cages for small animals lined one entire wall, filled with lush greenery which only seemed to exist inside Titus's lab anymore. The occupants were mostly monkeys, small ones. Titus didn't experiment on them... well, not until they were dead and their bodies cryofrozen. Then, he brought them back to life and healed them. He was reanimating a monkey he'd pulled from the freezer. She saw, from the label still hanging from the creature's toe, it had been dead for nearly a year. This was the challenge for Titus. Always older. Always more dead. It was possible for primates.

"He's cute," she said from the doorway.

A nearby chimp hopped around and signed, 'Me... choose me... choose me" at her.

"I'm not here to play, Frodo," she said to the chimp.

The chimp sat down in a huff and began grooming itself.

"Frodo has a crush on you." Titus glanced up to smile at her. His smile made her heart skip still. He pumped clear liquid through the chimp's body, warming the tissue in preparation for reanimation. "Did you mean what you said?"

"Yes."

He sighed and began setting tools out on a metal table nearby. He gestured at the monkey. "I've added some of the series five into the warming solution. This is my second small scale, but the one from a few days ago came from nearly two years post."

"Two years dead?" she asked, shocked. She looked around at the cages' occupants. Sure enough. A new monkey sat in one of the cages on the end, closest to Titus. The monkey folded a paper airplane. A stack of paper stood ready beside the cage and a horde of paper airplanes littered the nearby floor.

Titus smiled at her expression of surprise... and said to the monkey, "Show the pretty girl what you used to do, Chuck."

Chuck threw the paper airplane.

"I got him from NASA," Titus explained. "I'd planned to run some intelligence tests on him today, but I haven't gotten around to it yet." He turned back to the corpse he'd been working with. "I wanted to see if it was a fluke."

"A fluke?" she asked him, staring at the chimp. Chuck began folding a new airplane. How could Titus consider the chimp a fluke? Chuck grinned at her, showing her all his teeth and some of his gums. It was... charming... if you liked that kind of thing.

"I think he might be smarter than when he died... quite a bit smarter. Which is... well, opposite of what I expected. He also seems to... anticipate things happening. I broke a beaker yesterday by accident, and he went crazy just before it happened."

Chuck screeched and pointed at a light in the corner... moments before it flashed, alerting Titus that the chimp on his lab table had reached the correct temperature.

"See what I mean?" Titus asked.

"You've created a psychic, hyper-intelligent monkey?" she asked. "Sounds like you've created a monster to me."

Shrugging, Titus said, "I'm not planning on publishing these findings if I'm correct. It's... too far. I'm not ready to see this bastardized or taken to the next step. That's all we need is intelligent assassin zombies."

"Could Armand know about this? Maybe it's why he wants the series five."

"No... no way... you're the first person I've shown."

"Maybe he is spying on you... somehow," Mindy said.

They both looked around. No cameras... and no one was allowed in here besides Mindy... and the chimps, of course. Titus was a bit of a recluse all in all. She was the only one ever around his place.

"I don't see how. Besides, Armand always joked in school about how you never made anything smarter than yourself. I think he prefers his zombie drones because of it. Other than that one time two years ago, he stayed clear of reanimation of humans in a healthy way."

Titus rubbed the scarred portion of his left hand. She'd only recently heard the story of back when Armand and Titus were friends. Then, Armand had lost his wife in an accident and asked for Titus's help in bringing her back to life... but Armand's grief made him sloppy, and the whole lab nearly blew up. Despite what Titus might say to the contrary, he blamed himself for not checking the equipment. Back then, they'd needed to work fast, well... faster anyway. Really... they still needed to work fast if you hadn't gone through the immortality procedure. It basically stopped time. Time was irrelevant.

"Remember when we used to be scared of death," Titus murmured under his breath as he flooded the chimp's veins with a new solution and flipped the magnetic paddles to charge.

"Speak for yourself, Titus... some of us still are," she said.

"Then, why are you willing to trade?" Titus asked.

"I don't trust Armand."

"No, I don't either... but I'm not stopping your heart in exchange for this. You'd resent it," he said.

"I wouldn't," Mindy said... though she wasn't sure.

Titus picked up the paddles and pressed them on the chimp's head. "You would. Ask me again because it's what you want.... Ask me because you know it's what I want... but don't ask me to do this as a trade." The magnetic bolts shocked the chimp and pulsed through it. Almost immediately, the monitors beside the table flared to life. No heart rate... there wouldn't be one... but the brainwave activity spiked and the chimp opened its eyes.

"Welcome back to the world, Ace," Titus said to the chimp. Looking up at Mindy, he mouthed "It's alive."

She rolled her eyes.

Idiot. He was such an idiot. It was cute, but he was still an idiot.

She was following him, he could sense it. It wasn't too much of a jab at his masculinity that his girlfriend didn't think he could hand off this solution without getting injured. Well, it was, but he'd accepted she'd do it anyway. It was just as well, possibly, because a couple of Armand's henchmen... henchzombies approached him before he'd even reached the gates to Armand's estates. They'd moaned once and then found a crossbow bolt through their heads.

Mindy was good at what she did. She was lethal at nearly all distances... but she'd been following him closely this whole time. The zombies really hadn't stood a chance.

"Great shot," Titus called over his shoulder as he stood at the gate.

"Thanks," Mindy yelled back.

Armand's voice crackled over the old speaker box, "She stays outside."

"No," Mindy shouted from behind him.

Stubborn. The last thing he needed was to worry about her inside Armand's place.

"Okay," Titus responded.

Mindy growled behind him. He'd give her flowers or something... he'd reanimated a couple of orchids just recently. If she was an undead, he'd take her in with him, but that beating heart of hers was a liability inside Armand's estate. No. No way.

Taking out her aggression, Mindy shot a few more of Armand's henchmen who stood guard beside the front door. It probably was only a matter of time before they tried to kill her anyway... despite the trade he'd made with Armand. He didn't think his old friend would honor it, but it was worth a shot for Mindy's sake.

The gate swung open, and Titus called, "Be good, babe. Don't let them kill you until I get out."

She laughed and shot another zombie.

Armand's place was almost cliché in its super-villain motif. Stone floors with steel walls? Please, it was embarrassing. Armand met him with a crossbow at his shoulder aimed just beyond Titus's head. The bolt flew past his cheek and knocked down a zombie who'd been shuffling their way.

"How can you live like this?" Titus asked, glancing over his shoulder.

Two other zombies, more composed, dragged the dead zombie off slowly while moaning back and forth.

Armand shrugged. "Technically, I'm not living... and that one will keep them full for a few days before I have to kill another one who doesn't know its place."

"It's sick."

Armand raised his eyebrows. "Says the undead who is shagging someone with a beating heart. Hasn't anyone ever told her not to play with dead things?"

Titus held up the case. "What now, Armand? You've got me here out of curiosity, but if your freaks are outside attacking Mindy, I swear I'll let her in here to shoot your damn head off."

His old friend smiled. Titus never trusted Armand when he smiled.

"You've had a bit of a breakthrough, Titus… and I need you to push a button again." He gestured at a door. "Come. Follow me."

They walked into a lab much like Titus's reanimation lab… without all the signing chimps and living flora. On the lab table, with clear liquid running through a tube into her veins lay Armand's wife. He'd healed her, but her blank stare said he'd never gotten her past the zombie stage.

"I cryo-ed her until you'd reanimated Chuck," Armand said, gesturing at his wife.

"Chuck?" Armand knew about the chimp?

"Chuck has an implant in him. I got to him before you did. I figured when you'd done Chuck… you'd be ready. I've been throwing stuff at your girlfriend in the meantime to keep my negotiating options open."

Examining Lily, Armand's wife, Titus had to admit Armand had done an impressive job of healing her and prepping her for a zombie life. If her accident had happened more recently, Titus might have even contacted Armand about his success with series five. He and Armand had been close once after all. Lily had been a mess of limbs and blood and brain-dead for an hour when they got to her all those years ago. He'd been willing to try… especially when faced with Armand's desperation… but, chances were she would have been a vegetable with what they were using back then.

"I didn't know you saved her," Titus said. Armand must have rushed her into cryo rather than getting his shattered face dealt with after the explosion. That explained why the scarring had been so bad.

Lily moaned and fought against the restraints on her as the zombie solution's primitive animation took effect. Armand scanned through the documents Titus had brought in the case with the solution. Armand's plans started sinking in: inducing a zombie state… and then regenerating and healing the brain with series five. Armand led the industry in creating zombies. He regenerated entire armies of them for foreign countries to be used in wars. It was evil but brilliant… using it on his cryogenically frozen wife might just be brilliant.

"She was… is… my life," Armand said. "I figure with the series five on top of what I've done." Armand swallowed and looked at the door. "This doesn't leave this room, though. This would destroy my reputation. I'm planning a major coup, and it might not happen if they found out I've gone soft."

Titus laughed. "If I do this... if I help you... you'll stay away from Mindy?"

Armand rolled his eyes. "Your girlfriend has cut through my minions like they're still corpses. If you help me out, I'll be happy to find a nemesis with a less lethal girlfriend." He brushed a hand across his wife's struggling head. For a moment, he looked like Armand of old when he said, "You should still stop Mindy's heart, though. Once they die for real... well, you realize how much you've lost."

"Preaching to the choir," Titus said.

Armand snorted a laugh. "I also need a more devilish nemesis than you. Some days it's like kicking a zombie puppy. Squishy and your boots are covered in drool."

Titus nodded at the Lazarus machine beside the table. "You've cleaned the core."

"Yes, I've cleaned the core."

"You're sure about this? We've probably only got one shot at this... you can wait a few more months until I get some more large scale tests done."

"No... I'm worried her brain will decay if I have her on ice much longer... and, as she is... it's not Lily," Armand said, gesturing at the zombie who, in turn, snarled at him. No, it wasn't Lily. Lily had been brilliant and witty... and this was just a reanimated corpse.

It would have been good if Armand could see the correlation between his wife as she was now... and the zombies he created every day to be his minions ever since that fateful day in the lab... but that was probably too much to hope for.

"Okay, let's do this," Titus said.

Armand shut the door and set his crossbow beside it. "I swear, if you shout 'it's alive' I'll shoot you with my crossbow, though."

"Fair enough."

Mindy shot another one of Armand's henchmen in the head. Seriously... they just kept coming and coming. She'd heard Armand's estate sat on a graveyard which provided a seemingly endless supply of corpses to reanimate, but this was getting ridiculous. At some point, it wasn't fun anymore, you know?

Finally, after an hour... Titus walked out... sans the case full of series five solution. She'd been on the verge of launching an attack on Armand's fortress. Since he knew she was around, she might as well walk home with him.

Her crossbow in one hand as she scanned the area, she asked, "So, what did he want?"

"We had a... discussion about life or death," Titus said. "He won't be bothering you anymore... and I think he might shortly discover why you should, truly, never reanimate something smarter than you." Titus grinned. "I think he'd forgotten why we all laughed at him for marrying a Nobel winner."

"What?" Mindy asked. Sometimes Titus's brain ran away from him and he spouted nonsense. It was part of his charm, but it still didn't make any sense.

"Nothing," Titus said. He reached out his hand for hers and she took it eagerly. It did feel good to have this little confrontation over with, and maybe things would be less crazy if Armand kept his side of the bargain. "I'm sorry that took so long," he said. "It's a shame the buses don't run after dark... we're probably going to get attacked a few times before we get home."

Holding up her crossbow, she said, "I've got plenty of bolts." She cleared her throat. She'd had plenty of time to think about things while he was in with Armand. "I've been thinking... maybe it is time you stopped my heart." If anything had happened to him... she'd have lost her mind, so maybe it was time to accept he felt the same way. She wasn't being fair to him.

Titus glanced at her. "Really?" he asked, squeezing her hand.

She nodded.

"You're ready to join the army of the undead, huh?"

"After a really big meal," she said. And maybe not until after a week of really good dreams. "You swear it won't change the way you feel about me?"

"On my mother's grave."

Mindy rolled her eyes. "Your mother is undead and lives on the other side of town. She asked me to pick up some extra protein shakes for Thanksgiving dinner next week."

"She'd bought a grave... I just didn't see a reason for her to use it."

Mindy shot a zombie shuffling toward them. "Idiot."

"Me or him?" Titus asked.

She left that up to Titus to figure out.

Zombies & Religion: Necromancy
by RC Murphy

In this piece Zombie Survival Crew™ Commander RC Murphy takes a look at another real world, religion-based manifestation of society's fascination with the walking dead. Centuries of history teaches us to be wary of the necromancer. This knowledge bears witness to the power hungry that walk among us today, and raises questions around how far is too far for a modern practitioner.

☠ ☠ ☠ ☠ ☠

When one hears the word Necromancer you tend to envision a guy in his mid-forties sporting a cape and tux combo that would make Dracula drool in his coffin. We're talking someone like Doctor Orpheus from *The Venture Brothers*, here. The stereotype of a necromancer is outlandish, so ridiculous that we have a hard time believing people would call themselves one at any point in history. Which is a good thing. Playing with the dead isn't the smartest thing to do. Something always goes wrong.

Necromancy is a type of magic. Dark magic steeped in rituals used to call upon the dead. Some necromancers summon the spirits of the dead to predict the future. Others recover the corpse and "push" their magic into it, creating a zombie to control and communicate with. These rituals are long, exhausting, and involve sacrifices of blood. The amount of blood varies on the magic being conducted. Early necromancers believed that more was better. Accounts tell of practitioners standing before blood-drenched altars to work their craft.

During the early Middle Ages necromancy was fodder of both myths and reality. The Norse told tales of heroes contacting spirits of dead relatives to ask the dead to cast spells against their enemies. Another Norse saga tells of Skuld, a princess so skilled in magic and communicating with the dead that in the midst of battle she could force dead warriors to rise and continue their attacks. Skuld wielded and army of the undead, the likes of which we consider a big sign that the Zombiepocalypse is upon us. This undead army made her nearly invincible on the battlefield. A feat most men would be envious of and all feared.

Medieval necromancers believed that in order to raise the dead the Christian god had to be invoked during rituals. Because of this the majority of medieval necromancers were highly educated clergy members. There were few seminaries at the time. This made knowledge of Holy Scripture rare unless one was taught under an apprenticeship. The common man would not have access to the Bible. Nor would he be able to read the Latin it was written in. It was a long time before the printing press and the idea that every household should have a copy of the Bible in order to be closer to God. Necromancy became part of the Christian faith, a fact most would not admit.

At this time necromancers began to believe that they were not calling forth the souls of the dead to reanimate bodies, but demons instead. The soul was an object only God could manipulate, so they sought other explanations for the power they wielded. Demons were a great scapegoat. The Roman Catholic Church forbade members from practicing the dark magic for this reason. However enforcing the ruling was near impossible given the amount of time it took to deliver missives to other countries.

Despite the Church's declaration, necromancy was still widely practiced. Through time, necromancers used the stigma towards magic by Christian faithful to fuel their craft. Necromancers were hunted as witches, driven further underground to conduct their rituals and raise their dead. They twisted Holy Scripture, uttered names of demons never meant to be spoken by good, God-fearing people. Despite being based in reality, they became figures of legends and tales told to scare people back into church pews.

Modern necromancy has returned to the notion that they are communicating directly with souls of the dead. While some of the demonic influence still exists, it is more as a warning to practitioners.

Great care is taken to protect the area of ritual, usually with a circle of some sort to keep evil spirits (demonic forces) at bay. Necromancers nowadays typically aren't attempting to raise an army of undead from their graves. But do not disregard the idea. Power corrupts. Someone at some point will attempt to make an army of zombies through magic.

Hordes of undead under the control of a necromancer will move together. Unlike a typical group of zombies, these won't fight with each other while reaching for their goal or food source. Think of them as decaying marionettes. The necromancer will use their power over the dead to manipulate zombies to do their bidding. It could be anything from petty theft to a string of murders.

Because necromancy is a type of magic, there are repercussions to using the power. Sustaining control over the undead will drain them, leave them vulnerable to attack. If you can break the tie between zombie and necromancer, the zombie will return to the grave or attack the person that disturbed their rest. We suggest trying salt or salt water to do this. Salt in magic rituals purifies and will break down dark spells. If that fails, use fire. Zombie flambé, anyone?

Dead Man's Shoes
by Andrew Jack

Dead Man's Shoes follows a young man named Carlo when he wakes on the autopsy slab at his local hospital to find that the world has ended and zombies have taken the place of almost every human on the planet.

Almost.

Carlo meets up with Antoinette as he tries to escape, and discovers that not only does she have strange powers over the walking dead; she seems to know more about Carlo than he does.

As Antoinette brings Carlo closer to knowing the role he has to play in ending the apocalypse and saving the remnants of humanity, they are confronted by the demonic source of the plague, a creature named Legion.

To battle the demon, Carlo must confront his past, and call upon the Voodoo god of death, Baron Samedi, to fight for the future of mankind.

About the author:

Andrew Jack is a 29 year old writer living in Christchurch, New Zealand. He's been writing for most of his life, managing to collect his first rejection letter at the age of four. The publisher in question was very nice about suggesting he learn to read and write before resubmitting. A lifelong martial arts practitioner and a dreadfully bad shot, Andrew's chosen weapon of zombie destruction is the khukri, a forward curving knife originating in Nepal.

Andrew can be found conversing on a variety of subjects related to writing, current events and the dark arts on Twitter as @ajackwriting.

Dead Man's Shoes

Carlo woke up in the morgue. He'd been awakened by screaming, and the echoes of it crashed around in his head.

His muscles creaked as he rolled to the side on the examination table and sat, letting the sheet covering him fall away. Emergency lighting cast the room in halogen relief. He heard a soft, wet sound coming from behind the supply cupboard.

A woman crouched there. She wore a thin hospital gown, so slick with blood it clung to her body, accentuating what had once been beautiful. She crouched over the body of a heavyset man. She reached down and wrenched a chunk of red meat out of his chest, then shovelled it into her mouth.

Carlo gagged at the sight, and the corpse jerked her head up to look at him. Her eyes were milky white, and black veins stood out under the translucent skin on her face. She opened her mouth and hissed at him, a sound not even remotely human.

Trying not vomit, he back away and tripped over something solid on the floor. Another moving corpse, its mouth working soundlessly as he fell beside it. Carlo screamed and thrashed back to his feet. Tears streamed down his face as he took in the rest of the morgue. There were five bodies in all, all awake. Only the woman and the body on the floor moved, the others were tied to exam tables. Bloody clothing littered the floor, vaguely medical, in a bio hazard way. He didn't look too closely, afraid what the clothes might be covering.

The dead woman rose slowly, blood dribbling from her open mouth. Her head lolled to one side, and her filmy eyes didn't blink as she walked towards him.

"Get away from me, get…" Carl's dry throat reduced the words to a croak.

She growled, from somewhere deep inside her, and the rotting meat stink filled the air between them. Something was wrong with the way the woman walked, as if she hung from the wires of a drunk puppeteer.

He cringed away from her, driving his head back against the wall, his feet slipping in the blood on the floor.

She sniffed him, like a dog at suspicious roadkill, then she extended her swollen purple tongue and licked across his eye.

Carlo closed his eyes, feeling the dry rasp of her tongue scrape across his face, snagging his eyelid and dragging it open to see the veins creeping under her skin as she tasted him.

Just as Carlo thought he was going to pass out, she moved, lurching back to the body she'd been eating. The other bodies still mouthed and grasped at him, but as long as he kept to the walls, they couldn't touch him.

The terror stayed with him for so long Carlo began feeling detached. In a quiet corner of his mind he felt his heart trying to leap out of his throat, his rapid breathing and the sweat running off his face and mixing with the blood on the floor.

I have to get out.

It was the first thought that counted as a thought instead of a pure terror reaction. He started looking around for the door. *There.* Tantalisingly close, just past the rows of grasping hands.

Carlo took two deep breaths and charged as quickly as he could past the tied down bodies and into the double doors. A heavy chain held the doors closed. Carlo bounced off the doors and landed on his ass on the slick floor. He swore and pushed himself up to his feet. Carlo was a big guy, and he threw himself at the door again, aiming not at the chains but at the bolts holding the door to the frame. There was a loud crack, and the abused door tore out of the wall. Carlo entered the main hospital in a shower of splinters, just about running over a woman who'd appeared just to the right of the main door.

They stood blinking at each other.

"There you are. Do you have any idea how many morgues there are in this city?" Her eyes flicked behind him. "No, you stay where you are." She pointed a long white stick over Carlo's shoulder and unleashed a stream of words in a language that seemed oddly familiar to Carlo.

He turned to look at the zombie woman who stood behind him, her mouth hanging open. The creature stood transfixed by the woman in the hallway. There was a long second where Carlo thought the zombie would attack her, but she simply swayed in place for a few moments before grunting and turning back into the darkness.

The living woman in the hallway took a sharp step forwards and swiped the white stick, which looked a lot like a human thigh bone, over Carlo's forehead. "Give me a moment." She used the blood from his forehead to draw a quick, complex diagram on the ground in front of the broken door.

"What's going on?" Carlo took stock. He wore odd clothes; he looked almost like he'd dressed for a black tie wedding, assuming the wedding was being held somewhere very dirty. His pants and shoes were black and caked with dirt. The coat was also black, dirty and torn over the shoulders.

"Perhaps we should get away from the zombies first, then I can explain?" She was very tall, almost as tall as Carlo, who stooped to get through doorways.

"Can't you just…" he made a wand waving motion.

"On one or two, sure, the bone works. A big crowd though and even you're going to have to run." She started walking away from the morgue, skirting around the blood pools dotting the floor. A wheelchair stood empty, blocking one of the offices. A long, thick blood trail led towards one of the wards.

The hospital was still and hot, and the smell of rot clouded the air with flies. Carlo swiped at them as they strode through the maze of flickering lights and dark corridors. "What happened?"

"What does it look like?"

"Armageddon." Carlo felt sick. "The end of everything."

The woman smiled, creasing the smooth lines of her face. "Close enough, but maybe you and I can do something about it. Why do you think I was looking for you?"

Carlo shut his mouth. Memories that seemed to belong to someone else were floating through his mind. He remembered going to the movies with his wife, and that he liked ice cream with chocolate sauce. He didn't remember anything else except tiny snippets, images that came and went.

"This way." The woman opened a fire access door and started down the stairs. A security guard's body lay in the stairwell, a large silver revolver in his lap. The wall behind him was painted with the contents of his skull.

Carlo looked at the guard for a few moments, and then was heartily sick all over the side of the stairwell.

For a few moments all he could do was hang over the railing and breathe huge gulps of stale air. When he opened his eyes, the tall woman held out a hip flask out for him.

"Rum," said the woman. "It'll take the taste out of your mouth."

The flask felt warm in his hand. He took a swig, feeling the hot sweet liquid slide down his throat and warm his stomach. He immediately felt a little better, and took another drink, feeling the inscription on the flask as he did so. He angled the metal bottle into the light so he could see. "Your name's Camilla?"

"Camilla was my sister. I'm Antoinette." The woman took the flask back and took a long pull. She looked away from Carlo, then down at the floor.

"I'm sorry for your sister."

"As am I." She peered over the edge of the stairwell. "Come." She took the steps two at a time, her boots drumming out a steady rhythm that echoed back up the stairwell.

They passed a series of deep scratches in the wall, a single bloody fingernail buried a half inch into the deepest gouge. A few flights down were two large black doors. Sunlight streamed in through the dirty safety glass on each door, lighting up the back wall. One of the symbols Antoinette had drawn upstairs was painted large there; reminding Carlo of a tomb, surrounded by crosses and stars. It seemed incredibly familiar to him, but he couldn't have told anyone why.

"Here." Antoinette held out a battered looking pair of sunglasses to him. "The sun's bright out there."

He took them. "Uh…thanks?" They were the old aviator style glasses that wouldn't have looked out of place on the set of *Top Gun*.

She smiled and put on a pair of her own glasses. "You ready?"

"For what?"

Antoinette unbolted the door and threw it wide open, the handles on the other side banging into the outer walls. A sea of the dead looked back in at them.

Carlo's mouth hung open as the collected zombies all slowly turned to look. Hundreds of pairs of milky white eyes latched onto them.

One of the dead groaned. A long, drawn out sound, like someone slowly drawing the bow across a double bass. The others took it up, and the sound built and built until the windows rattled in their frames.

That's it, I'm dead. Carlo wondered what it was going to be like to be eaten. He felt oddly okay. At least he could stop being scared.

The sound died away. The dead hadn't moved.

"Come."

He staggered after Antoinette as she wandered among the walking corpses like she was picking her way through a field of statues. As they went the dead turned and followed them. Occasionally one of them would moan, and the cacophony would start all over again. None attacked.

"Where are we going?" The question Carlo really wanted to ask was 'what's going on?' but it seemed too big, so he asked small questions instead.

"Up," said Antoinette. She pointed ahead to a single skyscraper towering above the others around it. Her steps grew shorter and faster, and by the time they reached the main entrance Carlo had to jog to keep up with her.

He got so caught up in avoiding the shuffling zombies that the building's foyer took him by surprise. Dead bodies, flyblown and unmoving, were piled up around the entrance way. Bullet holes dotted the walls among huge congealed sprays of blood. The smell smashed him in the face so hard he retched.

Antoinette put a hand on his back. "Are you alright?"

"I'm really not. What in God's name happened here?"

She patted him gently. "The last group of the living were hiding here. They had many guns, lots of food, things were good. Then, slowly, they ran out of food, and then things got bad."

Carlo could see the events unfolding in his mind as she spoke. A small group safe high above the street, huddled on the top floor. He saw them getting thinner, and more desperate, until one day one day they decided they just had to hunt for more food. The streets were packed with the undead, and one of the survivors must have been bitten. They'd all agreed, if anyone one of them was infected, the others would kill them, quick and clean. But it was too hard, and the infected one offered instead to just walk outside, to just walk off and let the virus take them. And the survivors agreed, and they let the infected one go. But when they let that one go, they'd let the others in.

"You see?"

Carlo nodded. The smell still so strong he didn't trust himself to speak.

"Take this." She held out a thick cigar to him, another one in her hand. "Wish I had a gas mask, but these make things easier."

He took the cigar, letting her light one end with a black Zippo. He hadn't tried to smoke anything since high school when he'd been trying to impress a girl. He'd ended up having to go to sick bay because once he'd started coughing he couldn't stop. The cigars smoke was thick and pungent, but it masked the smell of rot that threatened to yank anything left in his stomach out through his nose.

Antoinette led him past the bodies in the foyer and to a set of lifts. Against all odds one still worked. The building must have had back up generators supplying power. The elevator even played a happy jingle as soon as they'd gotten in and hit the button that would take them to the roof. The smoke from their cigars filled the little space quickly. Through the haze Antoinette looked like a ghost, half real and half something else.

"What happens when we get to the roof?" he breathed in the thick smoke, marvelling at the way it felt as it slid into his lungs. He felt like he'd been smoking all his life.

"You'll know." Antoinette took the bag off her back and began rooting around inside. "You'll know."

"I'll know what?" He leaned back against the carpeted wall. The smoke got so thick he took off the dark glasses. Immediately he started coughing and the smoke got into his eyes.

"Put them back on." Antoinette hand flicked out and gripped his wrist forcing the glasses back on to his face.

Carlo stopped coughing.

He watched the smoke he breathed in swirling and eddying in the air. "That's... that's not normal."

Antoinette laughed, but didn't say anything. She pulled a large flat black disc of silk out of her backpack just as the elevator chimed and opened the doors.

It looked like people had lived there, and recently. It was also clear that anyone that had been alive there wasn't any more. Blood coated every available surface, from tiny speckles at the elevator doors to the bright splotch of red on the far wall.

A man stood in front of them. He was naked, and completely clean except for his hands, which were black with dried blood. He gave Carlo and Antoinette a little wave. "Hello."

Carlo stared. There was something wrong with the man's eyes, but he couldn't quite see what. He heard Antoinette hiss in a breath and press herself back into the elevator.

The man tilted his head to one side, a strong, insect like jerk of the head. "Hello?" Fresh red blood welled up underneath the caked scabs on his hands and began running in rivulets down his fingers.

"Uh, hi," said Carlo. He waved back with his cigar hand.

"Please come in, it's an honour to meet you Baron."

Baron? Thought Carlo, but he decided not to argue with the naked guy whose hands were dripping blood onto the carpet. He stepped inside.

Antoinette didn't move.

"Come in Antoinette, we mean you no harm." The man stepped across the carpet until he was a few feet from Carlo. His eyes roamed Carlo from head to toe and it became clear what was wrong with his eyes.

He had no eyelids.

Carlo was transfixed by the staring, bloodshot orbs that scanned him. He barely even noticed when the man started sniffing him.

The naked man suddenly laughed and clapped his hands. "A stand-in! you brought a stand-in for the Baron here? Oh Antoinette…" The grin on the man's face threatened to split his head in half. "Does he even know, or did you snatch him straight out of the morgue?"

Antoinette stood there, here eyes on the floor.

"Oh I'm sorry, how terribly rude." He turned the grin back to Carlo. "We are Legion. What name do you go by young man?"

"Carlo."

"A fine name, very fine. Tell me Carlo do you even have the slightest fucking clue as to what's going on? Do you?"

Silence filled the room.

Legion's smile belonged on a shark. "Your friend here brought you along to be a ride for an old god. She actually thought you'd be a good vessel. This building is built over a place of power, real power. Not that any of you fucking flesh bags knew." He flicked his hands, sending a shower of blood onto the floor. "So where is the Baron my dear?" He leaned in close, his voice becoming a stage whisper. "Between you and me, I don't think she expected me to be here."

Antoinette shook her head.

Legion leaned his head back, trying to get Carlo entirely into view. "Everything but the hat and the dirty jokes." He reached out a hand and the round circle of cloth flew out of Antoinette's hands and into his. He gave the circle a flick, and the top hat sprung into shape. "There we go. Have you ever met the Baron, Antoinette? Horrible man, if you can call him that, no class at all. Here, for what it's worth." He tossed the hat to Carlo, who caught it on reflex.

The hat was made of silk and a spring inside allowed it to be compressed. It tingled slightly in his hands.

"So, what shall we do with you?" Legion nodded behind them. "We could just eat you, but that lacks a certain poetry, and frankly Antoinette if it wasn't for you we'd have been bored rigid." He shrugged. "The apocalypse, who knew it'd be dull?" He sighed.

Carlo looked at the hat. What the hell. It sure couldn't hurt. He placed the hat on his head.

Legion looked at the hat. "Nothing?"

The hat tingled, making the hairs on the back of Carlo's neck stand on end. He felt like he was right next to something important. He turned his head to see if there was someone there. There was nothing but red smeared glass between him and the balcony.

He turned back just in time to feel Legion's fist close around his throat.

The lidless eyes bored into his, and Legion lips pulled back in a sneer as he walked towards the glass doors. "Do you remember your kids? I do."

An image flashed through Carlo's mind. A picnic with his wife and three squealing children. He remembered his wife's smile, broad and gentle. The image was so strong he barely felt Legion slowly drive him backwards through the glass door and outside.

"I said, do you remember them?" Legion reached a hand behind him, the blood flowing quickly off his hands and dripping onto the floor. There was a *thump* and the air around Antoinette rippled as she stepped through the broken glass. She froze there, suspended between the broken panes.

She stared at them, her eyes wide, and mouthed the word 'sorry'.

Me too, thought Carlo. He was still thinking about his family when Legion dangled his legs over the edge of the building.

The blood coming out of Legion's hand fell in fat red droplets into the fifty story void below. "Your wife..." Legion slapped Carlo with his free hand; it was like being clubbed with a sledgehammer. "Listen. Your wife was delicious." He let go.

Carlo fell. A droplet of Legion's blood fell next to him, a perfect red sphere. Light sparkled on its surface making it seem whole and solid. He stared at it right up until he hit the concrete. The light dimmed but didn't go out and Carlo saw himself standing next to a smashed pile of meat and bone. There was no other movement, even the shuffling zombies were frozen in mid stride.

Another man stood there in the strange dim light. He was tall, and had dark smooth skin, his eyes hidden behind dark glasses and the haze of smoke coming from the fat cigar in the man's mouth. The man smiled around the cigar, revealing perfectly white teeth lined up like tombstones in his mouth.

"So you'd be the Baron?" Carlo's voice felt strange, insubstantial. The droplet of blood that had fallen with him was frozen six inches above the pavement. The only thing that hadn't frozen was his body, which had completed its fall. Carlo knew it was his body, just as he knew the body he was standing in was his body too.

The baron bowed, his black silk top hat staying perfectly still on his head.

"How come I'm still alive?" The balcony seemed like a tiny dot, far above them.

"You dead." The Baron laughed. He had deep, smooth voice.

"What happens now?" Carlo looked up again.

"Normally I dig your grave, take your spirit to the next place. But Legion gone and changed things. Dead don't stay dead no more."

"The zombies?"

"Pfft, zombies. Not real zombies them, just corpses walking about. Got a little bit of Legion in 'em. Makes 'em mad." The Baron's smile dimmed. "I don't mind the dying, don't mind the real zombie but a world where they nothing but Legion…" The baron yawned, his mouth opening so wide it looked like he could swallow someone's head.

"So why don't you stop them?"

"Can't. Not my world, world of warm bodies. I can visit sometimes, but I can never stay." The baron picked up a shovel that had been buried blade first in the concrete. It came free with a *sching*. "How much you know about your Daddy?"

Carlo was silent for a long moment. "Are you trying to say you fucked my Mom?"

The Baron's laughter echoed around them. "I fucked your Momma, I fucked everyone's Momma. No one's Mom safe around Samedi!" He pulled a dirty bottle of rum out of his pocket and went to take a swig but found himself short one hand. He threw the shovel to Carlo so he could uncork the bottle.

Carlo caught the shovel and was driven to his knees by the weight. "Christ."

"He ain't here. You stuck with me." The Baron took a huge gulp of the rum, the smell of which drifted out of the bottle and floated through the air like fog. "And I'm stuck with you."

"What am I supposed to do?"

The Baron's smile vanished. "Choose."

"Choose what?"

"To live."

Carlo looked down at the burst sack that used to be his body. "I don't really think that's an option."

"Who you think you talking too? That just a scratch. Now you got to choose, can't keep you in between forever." He raised his eyebrows, tilting the hat on his head.

"Where's my wife? Where are my kids?" Carlo knew he should have been reeling with the revelation that his Dad was a chain smoking death god but all he could think of was Legion's bloodshot eyes boring into his.

"I don't know." The Baron stood very still.

"What do you mean you don't know? You have to fucking know, you're death right?"

"Don't be yelling at me boy." The rum vanished from the Baron's hand and he seemed much taller, the skin shrinking into his face. He loomed over had Carlo. "I mean they aren't in my domain, or Legion's. Means they still alive and not chewing on people. You should be grinning."

Relief washed through Carlo like a wave. It washed away just as quickly. "They're out there somewhere?"

"Yes. But we going to worry about that later. Time to work."

The Baron explained what he wanted. Carlo asked him to explain again.

"But I can barely lift this." Carlo proffered the shovel.

"You just a spirit right now. Can't lift shit."

Carlo looked down at his body. Bits of bone poked through the flesh like spears. "What happens if I don't do this?"

"Bad things." The baron had become almost completely skeletal.

"Worse than what's already happened?" Carlo looked around at the frozen zombies.

"Worse." The Baron pulled an ancient looking pocket watch from his suit. "Got to be now."

Carlo looked up straining his eyes to try and see the balcony far above. "Will it hurt?"

The Baron didn't say anything. Instead he reached into his jacket and took out the bottle of rum.

Carlo took it and took several long gulps. The raw rum burned every inch of the way down his throat and set a low fire in his stomach. The little part of him that still thought about such things wondered where the rum was going; his stomach was sitting, glistening, on the pavement.

He handed the bottle back to the Baron. "Let's do this."

The Baron took the bottle and gave a tiny nod. "Close your eyes."

Carlo closed his eyes.

Open.

The zombies were moving again. The closest one to Carlo gurgled at him and reached out. Carlo hit back with the shovel, marvelling at how light it had become. The Baron had sharpened the edges until it was less of a shovel and more of a gigantic broad bladed spear.

The zombie's head dropped to the pavement like a rotten coconut.

The gathered undead all opened their mouths and screamed, and the horde closed around Carlo as one being.

Skills that weren't his flowed through his arms, the shovel-spear dancing through the scrabbling screaming dead. Blood, black with rot, splashed onto the concrete.

Leave them. You wasting your time. The Baron's voice sat in the back of his head like a spider.

Carlo turned and ran towards the building. The street was filled with the dead, but not just the zombies. Strange translucent shades flitted around the walking corpses.

The spirits of the dead. They unhappy.

"No shit."

Wait. Don't go climbing no stairs. Legion coming to you.

He turned in time to see Legion land behind him, hitting the pavement so hard the lines of force spider-webbed through the concrete.

The blood dripping from his hands twisted and thickened into strange tendrils that covered his body and whipped at the air.

"Couldn't stay dead could you?" Legion's tendrils formed into barbs that fanned out around him like an angry squid. His lidless eyes had turned red and blood dripped out of them in long tendrils. Power radiated off him like heat, warping the air above into a mirage.

"Let's talk about my wife." Carlo raised the spear, trying to let Baron

Samedi's skills flow through him. He noticed out of the corner of his eyes the zombies had all stopped moving and were standing, watching them.

He focusing power. Can't control them and fight.

Legion was fast, God he was fast. Carlo retreated under a hail of blows, every strike he blocked let another through. He felt a dozen cuts burning under his clothes.

Carlo was losing. Even with all of the Baron's skill and power riding him the demon was too fast, too powerful. *I'm going to die.* Thought Carlo. *Again.* He screamed out loud as he thrust the spear out, but Legion simply ducked underneath and kicked his legs out from under him.

"I killed your friend." Legion kicked the spear out of his hands, sending it spiralling away into the sea of dead hands. He brought the same foot down on Carlo's arm grinding the heel down until the bone crunched. "I made it fast if that's any consolation." Legion smiled, letting the blood tears drip onto Carlo's face. They sizzled where they hit skin.

You got to fight. The Baron's voice seemed far away.

*I can't. My arm...*Carlo's thought disintegrated in a burst of pain.

You can. You just been too nice. He using a man's body. He got a few things he don't normally have.

"I think I'm going to let the children eat you. I think I'll enjoy that." Legion dragged one of the blood barbs across Carlo's chest, tearing through the material into the flesh below. "Does the great Baron Samedi have anything to say? Hmm?" He leaned down. "I beat you old man."

Carlo kicked out high and hard, his foot smashing into Legion's groin. The demon gave a surprised grunt and staggered backwards.

The Baron's voice came back with a howl of laughter that tore loose from Carlo's lips. "I think that sums up his thoughts on you. He say always remember the balls."

The Baron's presence roared in his mind. The spear appeared in his hand without a thought. For the first time he noticed the dead were watching him, not Legion. A deep low groan spread from one to the other. The ghosts shimmered in place, they seemed to be waiting.

They are yours. Speak to them. Speak! The demon will not be down forever.

He took a deep breath, and a voice both his and the Baron's boomed out into the crowd. "I see you all standing there. You will listen to me, because I AM TALKING."

Legion pulled himself to his feet. His features twisted into something almost wholly inhuman. The skin around his mouth tore as he screamed.

Carlo pointed the spear at the demon and addressed the waiting zombies. "Kill him."

As one being the zombies hit the demon, a tide of rotting bodies. Legion fought. Blood and gore flew and a pile of corpses began to grow around him. But the zombies kept coming, more and more poured from the side streets to launch themselves at him. One caught his arm and sank its teeth into him, another into his leg. His cry of rage became one of fear. He struck out with magic, dropping hundreds, but thousands had come to fight.

At the last moment Carlo felt Legion try and send his power out into the zombies, to regain control.

Now. The Baron's voice dropped low, his laughter gone. *Do it now.*

Carlo drew back the spear.

Legion held up a hand. "Wait."

"No." He threw the spear. It flew straight, hitting Legion between the eyes and shearing through his skull up to the shaft.

"Fuck," said Legion as he fell forwards, driving the spear right through. The creature's corpse twitched twice, and then began to rot, the flesh peeling away so quickly that there was little more than a skeleton left after a minute.

"Is it over?" Carlo asked the voice in his head.

Soon. Not yet. It is the spirit's time. The Baron didn't sound elated. He sounded grim. *They been waiting for this.*

Legion's spirit rose out of the bones of the body he'd once inhabited. It was a grey thing, hundreds of small blots in the air, distinct from the fluid shapes of the waiting ghosts. A face formed in the grey smoke and leered. A voice whispered in his ear about horrors yet to come.

Carlo said nothing. Instead he watched as the gathered ghosts fell upon the demon's spirit and tore Legion to pieces. Each ghost taking a tiny measure of revenge for the horrors he'd visited on their world.

After a moment, Legion was gone, as if he'd never been there at all.

Carlo fell to his knees, the Baron's power flowing away from him as quickly as it had come. A sob, all his own, shook his body. Another followed right behind. "What in the hell do I do now?"

A hand fell on his shoulder. He looked up into Antoinette's face.

"We have work to do." She smiled at him. "We've got to find your family for one."

"Legion said you were dead." Carlo laid a hand over hers and stood up.

"Demons. They're all liars." She glanced over his shoulder. "Speaking of liars."

The Baron stood behind them. The spear in his hand a shovel again. A fat cigar sat between his lips. "Sister. Take care of the boy." He looked at Carlo. "You not so bad. You call me." Then he laughed and took one long stride to left, vanishing into mid air, leaving a glowing hole behind him. The ghosts followed, flowing through the portal to wherever the Baron was taking them.

"What did you mean we've got work to do?"

"You don't think there's only one demon do you?"

Carlo had been hoping. "So I have to fight them all?" He sighed. "Well at least he left me an army." The zombies watched him with their filmy eyes. Waiting for instructions. He paused for a moment. Then turned to Antoinette. "You're his sister?"

"Ah now you see that's a long story." She smiled. "You're wife going to be somewhere West." She pointed towards away from the setting sun. "I'll tell you on the way."

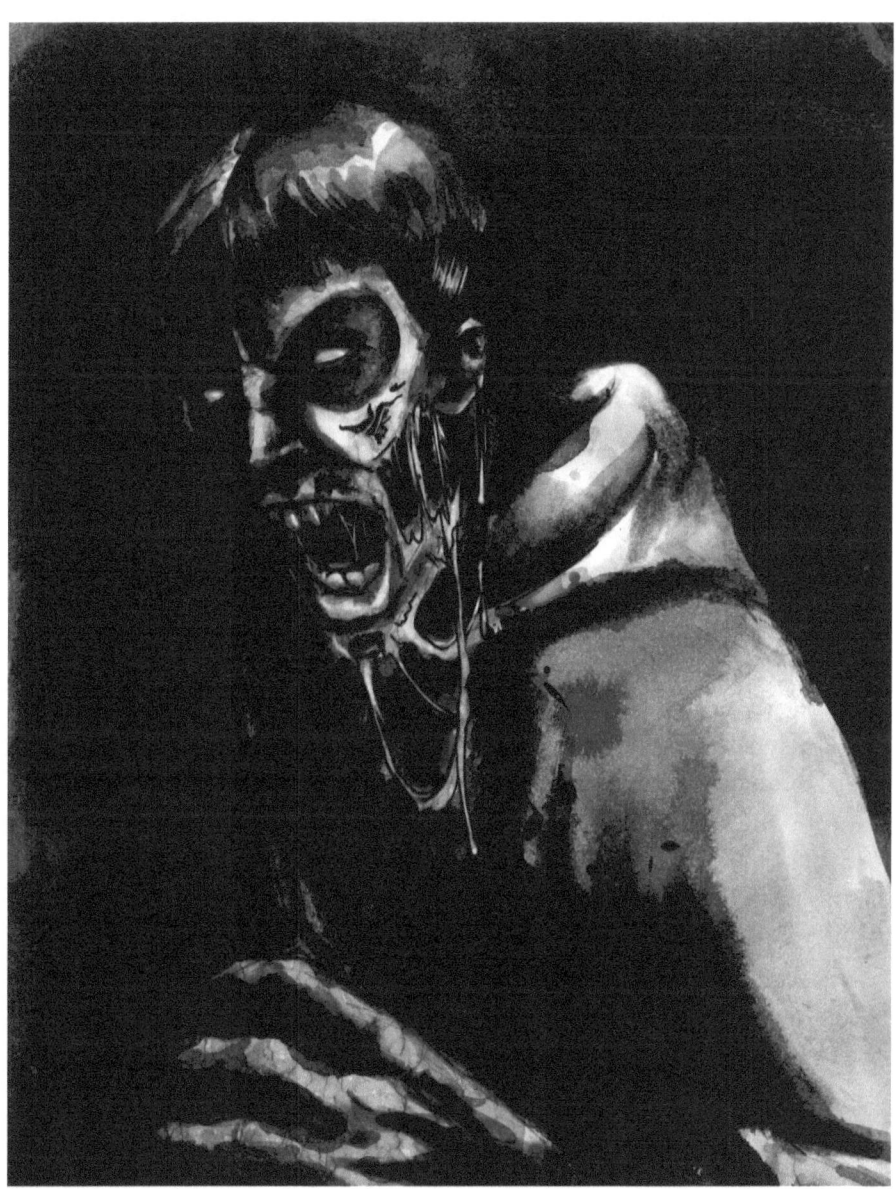

Never Say Die
by Gary James

A gentleman's club becomes a refuge for the well-to-do when the dead rise, through one member has a dark secret hanging over his head which threatens all who discover it. One by one the group's number dwindles, until there is nothing left to do but the unthinkable. This alternate history zombie tale recounts the final days in the life of one of the survivors, as his time - and the 1930s - draws to a dark close.

About the author:

Gary James remains shackled to the engine of commerce but dreams of a time when he can wander the earth delivering missives of wisdom and wit to the masses through his writing. From his home in the hinterlands of Scotland, Gary's lifelong love for horror works fails to prevent him from frequent genre-stumbles in his fiction and non-fiction writing – when he's not stumbling over the piles of books that infest his home. He has discovered, definitively, that books and coffee tables do not make good pillows. When he's not writing Gary is reading, painting, drawing or sculpting

Gary James on twitter: @BigWords88
Weapon of choice: Chainsaw

Never Say Die

The choir invisible isn't as invisible as it used to be; now streets chime with the tones of their number, and it seems their number grows every day. It is almost as if they have been drawn out into the streets from where they have fallen to join their fellow geaches in some macabre pack instinct unknowable to those of us whose eyes are still bright. Their irrepressible desire for the dark meat disturbs me in ways I have not the words to describe, though Asher seemed able to stand witness to their atrocities with no ill.

For the longest time I feared I would be ensconced within the walls of the Athenaeum forevermore, a living ghost who bore witness to the darkest of times. As there is little in the way of outstanding duties to perform, I have decided to use what time I have left to put to paper that which I know, and which I have done. Having had time to consider the alternatives, leaving this note - this memorial to events - is most likely the only way my story will be told. I can only hope some souls exist elsewhere in the city; that this is not in vain.

As days pass by unmourned and unmarked it becomes ever more evident to me my salvation is not to be. I have made peace with my eventual demise, and leave this testimony that some part of it may illuminate that which transpired here, as unbelievable as much of it must seem. You may scoff at my telling of events, for they are indeed incredible, but I am not a man of grand delusion nor fantasies. That you are reading this, that you have survived, is enough for me.

My name, if such things matter any more, is Lord Henry Abercrombie, though that was not my birth name. I was born in undistinguished circumstances, and by a mix of good fortune and cunning enterprise managed to make good of my existence. Public works may have sealed my reputation, but it was private financing where I truly made my mark, not least of which was scientific funding of up and coming men, visionaries the likes of which rarely achieve their fullest. It was not without some modicum of self-interest in which I bankrolled their endeavors, but I dealt fairly in both contract and company.

We were to be the architects of a bright new future. We were to be kings.

One of my protégés was a remarkable American named Weston, who had arrived in London after some scandal or other had disgraced him in the face of his Miskatonic peers. He had the most unique notions of chemical understanding, such that I had ever encountered, and was engaged in research in cataloging something or other which was beyond me. I was assured, from men of good standing, if he were to succeed there would be a pretty penny to be made in the use of such information.

But that was then.

Good fortune and cunning, as I have said, were my hallmarks. Both factors played in my favor on the morn of the twenty-first, as my ritual decreed I savored brandy and a Montecristo in the library on the second floor rather than in the reception rooms with the others. Asher was telling one of his stories about, I believe, some far-flung adventure. The disruption came at the ringing of the ten o'clock bell, with Fairfax staggering in claiming to have been assaulted by a most unkempt fellow. His arm was bloodied, and Caruthers - a fine practitioner of the medical arts - set to attendance.

The commotion outside soon became apparent, and the grand doors were closed almost immediately. I ventured down to see what assistance I could provide, but it was clear matters were well in hand. Beyond the confinement of the great club, however, the populace was busying themselves tearing at the walls of civilization. Never in my days had I thought to see Englishmen behave in such a fashion, for it was clear to all it wasn't the expected troublemakers, but good and honest people who were acting in such an undignified manner on the streets.

I hoped, in those early days, the malady gripping London was of some foreign machinations, as quick to dissipate as it was to rise.

Fairfax, who was often to be encountered expounding wildly, had retreated into a state of shock at his injury. Whilst seemingly superficial, it refused all manner of attempts to staunch the blood flow, and he quickly slipped into a fever which drew concern from Caruthers. Knowing so little of medical matters, I stayed out of the way. As day turned to evening his condition worsened, such that I thought at the time how strange it was to be privy to such a thing. It was troubling to see death's fingers grasp tightly around a fellow who - not two days before - had been the life and soul of any congregation.

Of my drinking companions, most were healthy young men. They were not averse to putting their shoulders into the work necessary to secure the club, nor to setting makeshift accommodations for what we supposed was the interim. The lower floor was evacuated for the more spacious upper floors, and the necessary accoutrements for a comfortable, if somewhat makeshift, stay were acquired from available resources. Parkinson set to making a meal, while Asher, undeniably of a strange temperament at the best of times, began to take watch over the streets from the balcony.

There were moments in those first hours that silent prayers echoed through me. The nightmarish ululations which rang through the streets set my jaw on edge.

The radio, which had been brought upstairs during the initial gathering of items, had been regurgitating static and half-formed sounds for most of the day. It briefly came alive as a newsman, in steadied tones more appropriate for announcing the weather, or giving the day's political events, made sure to inform all listening that it was important to stay indoors with the radio switched on in preparation for further announcements. It did not take long for the hiss and crackle to return to the speakers, even as the echoes of his words were fading.

Caruthers had been deathly pale since comprehending the extent of Fairfax's malaise, and as the day drew on he became more sanguine. It is my understanding their history goes back many years, to the fields of Ypres at least, if not earlier. I can only imagine the torment that must have played out in his mind as he watched the gradual deterioration of his longtime friend, with no way of alleviating the obvious suffering Fairfax was exposed to. Asher's offhand remark on bloodletting and leeches should have drawn my attention to his irrational mindset, but my own preoccupation had quite blinded me.

The numbing contemplation of my own mortality during those hours had been a drain on my good humor, and despite the dutiful ministrations of Parkinson - a Godsend, if ever there has been - the circumstances of the enforced siege had exhausted all reserves of energy. With both the telephone and the electrical telegraph inoperable, there was no means of knowing how long we would be forced to wait out calamities beyond our control. I retired to the billiards room, noting the cold compress applied to Fairfax's brow, and the worried looks of my companions.

When I awoke, little more than two hours later, Fairfax had passed on, though not without great commotion. The means of his death, as relayed to me later by a chap by the name of Hollister, was of some dispute. He appeared to flop to one side, which all agreed on, whereupon Caruthers attempted to pronounce him by means of taking his pulse. Disagreement arises as to the exact events immediately following this, as Fairfax - in his feverish delirium - was said to have lashed out, prompting Asher to raise a poker and set to him with murderous intent.

For the longest time there was silence, and much hostility aimed at Asher. He rebuffed all accusatory glances with what would become his customary manner.

We listened to the mute strains of the radio awhile, as theories about the situation were elaborated upon, and regrets were voiced by those young enough not to have any real regrets. The conversation was a maudlin one, and it soon became unbearable for us to continue with. That first night eight members fled into the darkness, with hopes that there were places untouched by the horrors visited upon us. There is no way to know what became of them, but I do not suppose they made a fair distance through the streets.

I made it known a headcount was to be established, and Parkinson, passing through the rooms on his butlerial duties, made note of thirty-two souls in our enforced residence, six of whom were present at Fairfax's demise. The days dragged on, with hot meals being brought up from the kitchen when necessary and drinks served when appropriate, Parkinson remaining vigilant in his record of our number. More than once it was required of him to protest at the suggestion of some contrivance to flee the grounds, and it eventually fell on Asher - once our group had dwindled to twelve remaining souls - to relocate all our appropriate duties, pastimes and constitutionals to a single room.

Living in close quarters with so many others, as one who has been in the service of our King will affirm, is no light matter, and our nerves were soon frayed beyond any could have imagined. Some of the arguments were entirely justified, though petty squabbles became aggrievances which spiraled out of control with remarkable speed. In removing the barriers we had surrounded ourselves with, the notion we should have been keeping track of the days slipped away. Not that counting off the days would have helped any. It was three or four days past Fairfax's last moments (a Saturday, or possibly Sunday) when Caruthers, so quietly we did not at first realize, died.

Parkinson made sure we were not inconvenienced more than necessary, removing traces of those who had departed, though the complete absence of our friends was made all the more apparent by the lack of their effects. In order to break the deathly silence, Parkinson turned the radio on again for us, and we listened as an announcer relayed what few facts surrounding the nightmare outside were then known. It became clear the authorities were very interested in speaking to Weston - when I heard his name uttered in relation to the sacking of the city by unnatural forces my blood chilled. I don't know if anyone noticed me taking my handkerchief to my face, but my shock must have attracted Asher's curiosity at that point.

Whittaker, an accountant of no more than thirty years of age, hung himself in despair.

Parkinson has been remonstrating with Asher to turn over an unused room to the side of the cloakroom for use in storing the bodies of the members who had met their demise on the grounds, but with little headway. Having no interest in keeping the shrouded bodies, friends or not, in the same building as myself, I deferred to a group vote when asked my opinion. It was concluded (much to Parkinson's dismay) that all remains should be removed from the premises in order to maintain good hygiene. During the undertaking of this most sombre task I noticed, to my great concern, Asher's absence.

My heart beat harder in those moments than I can scarcely remember.

Such a man does not go unnoticed, especially when recent outbursts had alerted all to his instability. I discovered him in the cloakroom, my personal diary in his hands. The fact that he would rifle through a fellow member's overcoat was bad enough, but to peruse at length such a personal document as a diary was beyond reproach. I confronted him there and then, but his reaction was most unexpected. Having the gall to read my private thoughts was not enough - he laid out accusations of such a nature that I can no more repeat them here than I can explain that which came over me.

In anger, and the heat of the moment, we fought. Parkinson, loyal to the end, attempted to separate us. Asher, darkened with rage, turned on him and threw him bodily across the room - it was a dire act, for Parkinson, too stunned at the assault to steady himself, fell headfirst into the edge of the door. With so much death surrounding me, and fearing the worst from Asher, I grabbed the nearest object with which I could protect myself. I will never forget the sound of the cane as it struck him. As it rebounded off his skull, and made contact again. And again. It must have been a full two minutes before I came to my senses.

Good fortune and cunning. My blessing and my curse.

I did not know the two remaining fellows well enough to confide in them the full tale of what happened downstairs. In truth, I am probably too ashamed of my part in things to ever reveal to them the complete account of all which passed. My sins will be answered for soon enough. The matter has already been settled in my mind, but I will wait until nightfall to make my atonement. It should only be a matter of force to pry open the door, after which the geaches can have all they want of me. I have brought this upon us all, and it is only right I not outlive the others. If only I had held back the funding of Weston's diabolical experiments.

If only...

I didn't mean for this. I didn't mean for any of this. Weston's experimentation was meant to be purely in the realm of the theoretical, not this.

Not the raising of the dead.

I have damned us all. I have damned us all to Hell.

All of us...

We Take Care of Our Own
by EC

To ZSC Brigade leaders and 1st Lieutenants:

I'm sending this from a tiny town outside Moab called End of The Line. I've holed up in an Old West museum with a Navajo named Joe Holiday. The walkers have thinned out, but that won't last long. I've had a lot of time on my hands, so-

We Take Care of Our Own is about a tight-knit family dealing with survival admidst the Zombie Apocalypse in a small Midwestern town and was inspired by the *The Walking Dead*. The treatment of both the graphic novel and the TV series inspired this tale because it's brilliantly complex, poignant, and shockingly real. *We Take Care Of Our Own* examines the human reaction in the shadow of the Zombie Apocalypse.

I'll be moving on in the morning with Joe. We'll be heading to Monument Valley, where his people are. In the meantime, keep up the good fight...I know I will.

About the Author:

EC grew up in the small Midwestern town of Streator, Illinois, where he found himself escaping into the fictional worlds of Edgar Allan Poe, who led him to H.P. Lovecraft, and finally, Stephen King.

EC majored in English and minored in Poetry and has worked in Hollywood, where he wrote and directed episodes of the hit TV show SCRUBS and learned the craft of writing.

While on *Scrubs*, EC wrote episode 504 *"My Own Personal Hell"* and directed Episode 912 *"Our Driving Issues"*. He also wrote and directed a short film starring Zach Braff entitled *"5 Minutes to Midnight"*.

More recently, EC has begun re-writing a script originally written by the Father of the Zombie Genre himself, George Romero, and is also developing a Western screenplay he wrote with collaborator Blu Murray that gained them the attachment of Sam Elliott. Look for him on Twitter as @EC_Stories.

Weapon(s) of choice: Two Colt Frontier Six-shooters (they were my Grandfather's) and a Remington 1100 semi-automatic shotgun.

We Take Care Of Our Own

My brother and I are the only two left in Churchville, Illinois, population once 112. I'd say last two alive, but that's not really right. I'm alive, but my brother, Tom Nolan, is very dead. He's a zombie now. An undead man walking. Tom used to call them flesh-heads, like the towel-heads he fought over in Iraq, but that was before he got bit. I know I'm supposed to put him down, but he's my brother, and we promised Dad that we'd take care of each other no matter what.

Dad always said, *"Us Nolans, we take care of our own."*

It's the six hundred and sixty-sixth day since we stopped using calendars. I only know because 665 is written on the little chalkboard I keep up here. Beneath it are the thin remnants of all the numbers that have been written and erased. I take up the nub of chalk, erase the 5 with my finger, and draw a 6 in a looping motion.

666...the number of the beast. I think of the Iron Maiden song. It was one of my brother's favorites. I remember their mascot, Eddie; tight dead skin pulled over his skull face. In one of their posters Eddie was dressed like Uncle Sam, grinning and pointing his rotten knife of finger. That's right; UNCLE EDDIE WANTS TO EAT YOU! Welcome to The Zombified States of America!

I lie still for a minute, breathing in the warm attic air; wood and dust, mixed with my own stink. I've long taken to sleeping in my clothes. Tom used to say they'd stand up on their own if I bothered to take them off. I don't sleep very well anymore. Mostly because my mind always goes back over all the things that have happened, and partly because of the Metallica that plays all night long. I play it for Tom, and for me. They were his favorite band, and it helps to drown out the racket he makes the minute darkness falls. I don't know what it is with flesh-heads, but the night wakes them up, like rats or coyotes; gets their zombie engines runnin' full throttle and sharpens their senses. Even though Tom is walled up in Grandpa's bomb shelter, he always knows when night has come.

I sit up on my mattress. My butt sinks down through whiny, shot springs to the wooden floor beneath. The emptiness in my stomach howls. Man, I'm hungry. Maybe I'll find some food today in town. Maybe.

The lone window in the attic glows white hot with sunlight that blots out Illinois farm country below and beyond.

I pull on my boots, and remember buying them with Dad and my brother. I reach for my brother's belt and stand up, careful not to whack my head on the low eaves thick with shadows and cobwebs. I thread the belt into my jean loops, and pulling it tight, see I've punched six new holes in its cracked leather. My brother used to say I looked like one of those starving children on TV.

I take up my shotgun that stands against the wall like a cowboy leaning on a post. It's a Remington 870 express pump action. Dad gave it to me when I turned thirteen. I'm seventeen now, and I miss being thirteen something terrible.

I start down the attic steps, each one creaking its own note like piano keys.

The basement is cool and dark as a moonless field. Morning quiets my brother, and all the Metallica albums on the mp3 player usually run out about four in the morning.

I snatch the mp3 player, with its cracked plastic face, out of the speakers it spends the nights docked in. Mom gave us the mp3 player and the speakers. She bought them right after she got herself a eBook reader. Mom said we shouldn't be afraid of technology, especially if it helped a person appreciate the arts. I guess Metallica, Tom Petty, and Bruce Springsteen are as much art as Mom's books.

I stare for a moment at the thick steel door that keeps my brother safe. I touch my hand to it, wishing I could still touch my brother. I wish I could still muss his hair, or try and make him flinch. He stirs behind the door. I hear the slow clicking and clacking of his teeth, tired from gnashing all night, followed by a low, growling grunt, then silence. I slip the mp3 player into the front pocket of my jeans and bound up the steps, thinking of Mom instead of my zombie brother.

The sunlight leaks into the kitchen around the edges of the ply boards that cover every window on the first and second floor. I hate it because it makes the whole house feel like a cardboard box, lit by seams and cracks, but without them, there'd only be a pane of glass between you and death. Not that plywood keeps death out, 'cause it doesn't, but it's a good first line of defense.

I set my rifle on the kitchen table, next to the boxes of shells, and go to my bike angled against the counter. I check its chain and return to the table. Man, I'm tired. I sit down. Just for a minute.

Soon enough, I'll go into town and look for food and survivors. That's the routine, and Dad used to always say, *"Keep a routine, and it'll keep you."* Dad was high on routines because he had been in the army. We Nolan men are two things, soldiers and farmers. Grandpa Dale, who I'm named after, fought in the Pacific during WW II. Dad served the Big Red One in Vietnam; two tours of duty and one Purple Heart. Tom was a Marine, and went to Iraq for the first Desert Storm. I planned on enlisting after I turned eighteen, but Tom said I got drafted into this fight.

"The American fight for survival," Tom would say. Crock of shit if you ask me.

Dad would always talk about how as things got worse, routines would save us. It was like my favorite book. It's about a group of kids in military school who end up stranded on an island. At first they try to do things the way they know how, but little by little, kids do what they want and stop sticking to the routine, and go wild. Things fall apart, like what happened with our family and the people in town.

I want to get up and go outside, but I know I can't. Not just yet. Not before I remember the last time that Mom, Dad, and Tom and I were all together. It was right here in this kitchen where I now sit alone. The loneliness swirls around me like a thick ground mist full of memories.

I try to make myself get up, but I don't want to. I want to remember.

I see Mom and Dad at the table, while my brother and I lean against the counter. The kitchen swims with light, back then we hadn't boarded up all the windows yet. Mom's asking Dad to go to a town meeting he doesn't see the point in going to, because whatever is said there won't change his mind.

"It's springtime, Helen. Every trip into town is a risk," Dad says.

Mom knows this, but she says they'll be careful like they always are, and all he has to do is listen. Mostly, she just wants the town and all her friends to understand that our family isn't being selfish like everyone thinks. Even though once a small town's made up its mind it's a nearly impossible thing to change it. Mom says they're just scared like everyone else.

"I don't care about anyone else, Helen. I care about you and the boys. All I can do is take care of my own," he says.

Mom takes his big hands in hers, and just stares at him. Mom had a way of smiling at you when you were mad or feeling down, and sooner than later, you'd be smiling right along with her. Her golden hair hung around her face, and she wore one of her dresses, yellow with blue flowers floating on the fabric.

Soon enough, Dad smiled, and said, "You know you got sunshine in your veins, Helen."

She laughed and said, "Better than the ice water in yours, dear."

"What's that supposed to mean?"

Mom stood up and swept behind him, her arms falling around his shoulders, and then she said, "You know I like the strong, silent type, Bill." We went into town that night for the meeting, and it all went wrong, just like I think Dad knew it would.

That was a year ago, and I'm glad I can still remember them.

I step off the porch into the day. The sky is a high, bright blue sea today, not the low grey ceiling it's been for months. The barn swallows sing somewhere in the distance. Spring is here again. Spring is good and bad, good because it won't be so damn cold from now on, and bad because spring is when the dead get to wandering far and wide. The first year, when winter came, the flesh-heads were scarce. Dad, Tom, and I all took a ride in Betsy, our old Suburban, and then we found out why. We found a mess of them frozen solid with crows perched on their iced limbs. We heard in the cities they hole up in blown-out buildings. Some even make their way down into the sewers. Out here there's nowhere to go. Then when spring comes along, they thaw, and get right back to looking for us. They hunt through the dandelion summers and the Halloween times, right up to when we celebrate cheating the Indians with Turkey and stuffing. All the best months belong to the dead now.

I'm listening to Tom Petty while I ride toward town. It's about six miles from our farm to Churchville. Funny name for a town, huh? You'll know why soon enough.

Tom Petty's guitar whines and wow-wow's in my ear.

I peddle past Bob Volkman's gas station, looking up at its sign. It screams NO MORE FUCKIN' GAS, PLEASE STAY AWAY scrawled in black spray paint over VOLKMAN'S FUELING STATION. I see myself floating by in the shattered windows of the station. I'm all skin and bones staring back. Bob lost his head when things got bad. Actually, he blew it off. People in town doing things like that always made Dad real sad, but what really worried him was the whole town losing its own head. Right from the start, Dad said soon enough people would start to turn on each other. He was right and wrong. They turned all right, but on the Nolan Family.

I try to forget by listening to Tom Petty.

Something's moving up ahead. I sit up in my seat, braking; my tires hiss and grab the road. I stop my mp3 player. The slack line of my senses pulls tight, bit by a big fish deep down inside me.

It's standing up close to the green metal square of a sign that reads CHURCHVILLE, POP: 112 in reflective lettering. Once. Once, it was.

It's the first zombie I've seen in two months, and I think I know him.

I set my bike down at a distance, and unsling my shotgun.

He's still wearing a Streator High School letterman jacket. There isn't a school in Churchville, so kids go to Streator or Oakland. My brother and I went to Streator. Oakland has black jackets with silver trim, just like the football team in California. Streator was the bulldogs, and had red jackets with white trim.

This zombie isn't wearing pants. No siree-bob, just underpants that are way past yellow. His long bare legs end in a pair of cowboy boots. Not like my redwings, but Fancy, embroidered ones. On the sleeve of his jacket, crusted thick with blood, I make out the number one.

"Chad Kirby," I say out loud. My throat is dry and tight, and I cough the words out in a whisper. Chad was one of those guys who used to have it all. Quarterback and Captain of the football team, along with Tricia Keen, cheerleader Queen, and honor student, on his arm. Now he's a pantsless flesh-head.

I wonder how he lost his pants. Maybe Chad was in the backseat of his mustang trying to get it on with Tricia when the zombies came. Did he just run, leaving poor little Tricia to fend for herself?

He doesn't notice me, but that's because I haven't made any noise yet. Zombies hunt for sound more than anything else. I raise my shotgun and shout.

"Hey Kirby, you can't throw for shit." He lurches forward, banging his head on the sign. He rolls off it, turning with his whole body like Boris Karloff in those old Mummy movies. His milky eyes roll in his head before settling on me. He shuffles in my direction. His lipless mouth is a tattered hole lined with skull-teeth chomping up and down, making a TAK-TAK-TAK sound. The splintered end of his broken collarbone pokes out through the shoulder of his letterman. It makes his right arm useless; his throwing arm. That's pretty fuckin' funny. After awhile you can't but find the humor in it.

The other arm jerks upward, fingers clawing on the air.

I pump my shotgun, chambering the shell with a loud *shuck-shuck.*

I should just pull the trigger, but this has never been easy for me. Dad used to say, *"Every zombie used to be someone."* Chad probably doesn't even know why he's here, but I'm sure the sign is what brought him. Zombies always come back to places and things that used to mean something to them before they got dead.

I'm backing up as Chad's feet scuff along the ground kicking up tiny dust devils. TAK-TAK-TAK go his teeth, faster and faster. I can see his green, puffy tongue rolling around inside his mouth. It's funny how slow most flesh-heads are. My brother and I used to watch zombie movies before all this. We'd argue which movies we liked best, and what kind of zombies we thought were coolest. My brother liked the Romero zombies—George Romero, that is—from movies like *Night of the Living Dead,* and *Dawn of the Dead*—the original. They're the slow-walking zombies. I liked the new zombies, like the ones in *28 Days Later.* They're the fast zombies. Turns out, Romero was right. Real zombies don't run at all. Slow and steady wins the race, like that bedtime story mom used to read me about the tortoise and the hare.

Chad Kirby opens his mouth real wide, so wide it creaks, and lets loose with a rasping, retching noise, and then he belches up a boiling cloud of gnats. I finally pull the trigger, and paint the Churchville sign with his brains. It spreads out like thrown paint, bits of skull sledding down through the blood running to the bottom edge where it drips into drops.

I kick the dirt up into a small dusty breath. *Why'd you have to go and become a flesh-head, Chad Kirby? Why'd you have to make me blow your brains out?* I can pretty much remember all the zombies I've ever shot.

That's the thing with zombies and small towns. In the cities, where it started, it's herds of people, and most of them don't know each other. Out here, in a prairie town of a hundred or so, everyone knows everyone. It's a hell of a lot harder putting down people you know. Like your bus driver, or your dentist, or… I think of my brother.

Dad used to always say you couldn't fault a zombie for what it did. He'd say zombies are like rabid dogs. When a person got bit, it was that zombie engine driving them at you. Sure, they need to be put down, but you have to do it right. One time, Dad said, "*What if it was me boys.*" Tom said he would put Dad down if he had to, but things like that are always tougher than you think.

I look toward town. The three steeples of Churchville stab the blue sky so it looks like it's bleeding swirls of white, wispy clouds. I put my mp3 player back on, and hit shuffle.

Bruce Springsteen sings about a state trooper.

I roll my bike forward. My right foot pushes down and pulls me away from Chad Kirby's body, dead for the second and last time.

Bruce sings about brothers and family. I think of Mom and Dad, and my brother again, and I realize I'm crying. I'm glad my brother isn't around to see me cry like this, but I don't care because right now crying doesn't feel half bad. I'm so goddamn hungry. I wonder if my brother is too. I know he's hungry for other things, but I wonder if it hurts like my stomach hurts?

And the Boss sings on.

Churchville is what you might call Podunk, USA, or Bumfuck, Nowhere. The road I'm on, Illinois Route 18, cuts through Churchville, into Kingsville and the town of Cain, and all the way to Streator. It's all Vermillion County, on account of the Vermillion River; big dirty brown snake of a prairie river.

It's a nice kind of quiet this morning. There's a real soft wind blowing. It sounds like a far away whisper, and feels like when Mindy Hart blew on my neck once. I turn my mp3 player off in town. You need to stay alert out here. Plenty of people died because they let their guard down for an instant.

I ride past the old farmhouses where the few rich people in Churchville used to live. Dr. Goss's big old rambler with its wraparound porch, and Bill Cotter's spread. Bill Cotter's family founded Churchville, and they, which meant Bill, ended up owning most of the farmland around these parts, along with land all over Vermilion County. Doesn't do him any good now that he's dead. Land and money don't mean much at the end of the world. The rich are right back down with the rest of us when that comes. Dr. Goss and Bill Cotter, along with Reverend Shaw, lined up against Dad when things got bad between the town and us.

Up ahead is the Churchville Sheriff's Station. It isn't really much of a station, more of a red brick box. I remember Sheriff Wayne because of how he tried to save Mom that night. Sheriff Wayne was tall and wide, with his big broom of a mustache. He was a good man.

Next up are the skeletons of the drug store and Post Office, and the grocery store, or *Country Market*, like its sign says. Their windows all boarded up like one of those summer towns in winter. For awhile their owners, who were all from Churchville, holed up inside. Eventually they moved into the churches because Reverend Shaw said there was strength in numbers. Dad said Reverend Shaw just wanted other people to watch his ass because he sure as shit couldn't do it for himself.

I stop in the center of town, looking up at the three churches of Churchville. You get it now, I bet.

St. Anthony's Catholic Church, St. Paul's Evangelical Lutheran Church, and the Third Baptist Church of Churchville. It was Bill Cotter's great, great Grandpa who settled Churchville. Supposedly, he was some kind of bible salesman. As the story goes, he rode through this patch of land in eighteen hundred and whatever, and had a vision from the lord, or an idea for money, Dad always said.

Old Man Cotter thought the best way to get people to move to a place might be churches. He was certainly wrong on that one. People came to church, and kept coming for many years, but businesses never followed. Churchville was a place where people went to church, but that was about it.

Above me, crows spot the blue sky in flapping, squawking silhouettes, and come to rest on the churches like buzzards on bones. St. Anthony's façade is grimy and grey with filth. Its steeple's black clock eye stares down at me, white hands stopped at one-thirty two. St. Paul's white-painted skin is blistered and peeling; blackbirds sit thick on its face like stadium spectators. Finally, there's Third Baptist, looking like a red brick Cyclops sitting Indian-style. Its square face rises up to a gaping round hole where a stained glass window used to be. When Reverend Shaw declared Third Baptist the "town headquarters," they punched out that window and put men with guns up there. Dad asked the Reverend if it occurred to him that knocking out that window would turn the church into a walk-in freezer come winter. It had not. Dad said times like these were ripe for false prophets.

I step into the quiet of the church, light streaming down through dust whirling like snow into a bright white circle on the pulpit. Rubble crunches under my boots, and birds burst upwards and downwards from all the quiet roosts.

I move through the warm slant of light, into the shadows of the church, and take a seat in the front row. A misty wind blows through my mind.

This is why I really come into town these days; to remember that night. Remember Dad and Mom. Even if it's a terrible memory, it's the last one I have of them, and so I let myself go back there.

After the second winter, with spring just around the corner, that Reverend Shaw started in on Dad at the town meetings. The Reverend thought that Dad ought to let all the survivors left in town move onto our farm. The Reverend said, *that farm is God's farm*, and Dad just said, *I will gladly tell God that it's Helen and Bill Nolan's farm, Reverend.* After all, we had the most food in storage, more guns than most, and more space than anyone with our house, barn, and stables. Dad said he understood where the Reverend was coming from, but that he just didn't want that kind of responsibility. Dad was happy to keep sharing our stores of food, like we were already doing, but his only real responsibility was to his own family.

We take care of our own.

The Reverend blew his top. He yelled at Dad, spit flying out of his mouth. "It's spring, Bill! You know those things will be coming through here in droves soon enough!"

"And this Church has held through some mean moments, and it'll do the same this spring," Dad said.

"God is watching you, Bill Nolan, and he is ashamed!" That's when Dad shot the Reverend a stare that reminded me of Clint Eastwood in those westerns. His lips got tight, and his eyes narrowed. Dad stepped forward, his nose almost touching the Reverend's, who was shaking where he stood with clenched fists that looked like doll's hands, small and useless.

Then Dad said, "In case you haven't noticed, Reverend. God is on vacation, and by the time he clocks back in, we'll all be gone. So if anyone should ashamed, it's that bastard sitting on high in heaven. You're asking too much of me. I'm sorry." Dad turned again on his boot heels, signaling to us that it was time leave, when the Reverend shouted after him.

"What about that bomb shelter of yours!?!"

"Reverend, there's twenty people in this church right now, and that shelter is ten by ten feet. There. Isn't. Enough. Room."

Dad wasn't lying. Grandpa built it during what he'd called the Red Scare. Before it held my zombie brother, it was just a place for Dad to store things away, and for Tom and I to play in from time to time. Once, Tom got mad at me for cheating at cards—I wasn't—and threw me in there with the door shut. It reminded me of that story in the bible, when Jonah gets swallowed by the whale. The dark was so thick you felt upside down, and the air didn't move in there. It was hardly a place for one person, let alone a whole church full.

People we'd known for years gathered into an angry flock behind the Reverend; they shouted and yelled, and some of the women even started to cry. Mom tried to calm everyone down, but no one heard her. She pleaded with Dad, but he was steaming mad at this point. She took his arm, and he snapped at her.

"Dammit, Helen! You asked me to come here tonight, and I did. But it doesn't change one bit how I feel. All I care about is YOU…and the BOYS, do you understand me?"

I think Mom understood, but she was always looking for a way to meet everyone halfway. Of course, I don't think halfway really ever works. Mostly, it seems like it's all or nothing in this world.

Dad knew if he let everyone come to the farm, it wouldn't be ours anymore. It would be the town's. And other people weighing in on what we did, and how we did it.

Mom thought it might be nice to have other people around; it would be like taking in a family of orphans. "*And THAT is a good thing, Bill Nolan,*" she said.

I thought about offering up my bedroom to Jenny Sherman, because I had a crush on her since kindergarten.

Dad knew it would only make things harder. He was determined to keep things simple, keep things under control. I think Dad forgot that in these times, the dead times, there was no controlling anything. It was only a matter of time before things happened to us just like everyone else.

Dad leaned down, and told me to go start the truck.

I was in such a hurry to do what he told me, I didn't bother to check the wide dark that wrapped all around the church. I made a beeline for Betsy, got inside, and started her up. I remembered not to turn the headlights on right away. That was a good way to ring the dinner bell for the flesh-heads, but so was starting a big old diesel Suburban in the dark.

Dad stormed out of the church ahead of Mom, and I turned on the headlights. They lit up a forest of zombies I had not seen standing in the dark. They were waiting. Mom didn't see her old bridge buddy, Carol Berry, step out of the shadows by the church doors. Her mouth was a bloody, biting hole in the middle of her swollen, waxy dead face. Carol grabbed Mom's shoulders, and then it all happened like an old time movie, rushes of jerky motion and slow-moving moments. The headlights cast their long beams through the murky night air, lighting up the front of the church. Betsy had become a projector, throwing a horror show up on the black screen of night.

Dad ran to help Mom while she fought off Carol's mauling mouth. The flesh-heads surged. Mom broke free, tried to run down the steps, but her feet found no footing. She tumbled down into their arms like a rock star crowd surfing. I saw her scream as their hands swelled up around her, pulling her down into their heaving, swaying pack.

Tom screamed and squeezed the trigger of his Winchester Model 70 whenever he had a clean shot; the tops of zombie heads exploding in smoking chunks into the air. I can still hear those thirty-aught-six cartridges cracking on the air.

Sheriff Wayne roared from the church like a linebacker on a blitz run. He knocked flesh-heads over left and right, screaming as he drove into the pile that engulfed Mom, "You dead sons of bitches! You dead sons of bitches! You dead sons-..." His words were bit right in half, and then he screamed as if he were caught in a great whirring piece of machinery. The scream rose higher and higher, becoming an awful screeching, vibrating sound.

Dad was right behind him, reaching for Mom. His eyes went wide, his mouth a soundless circle, then Tom yanked Dad out by his jacket and dragged him back to our truck. Dad tried to break free, his hand sprinkling blood in a wheeling wet web as he swung it through the air. Tom punched Dad hard, knocking him still against Betsy. Finally, Tom flung the back door open, threw Dad in like a sack of grain, and dove in after him.

"Drive, Dale! Goddammit, DRIVE! DRIVE! DRIVE!"

I stomped on the gas so hard I thought Betsy might flip herself over.

Her tires spun and screamed on Main Street; she lurched forward, mowing the clamoring dead down and sucking them underneath in a grinding circle.

In the rearview mirror, Dad laid in Tom's lap holding his blood-slicked hand to his chest, crying and muttering to himself.

"I saw her...down there. I saw her eyes. She looked up at me. I couldn't...I couldn't get to her...couldn't get to her...I'm so sorry, Helen. I just couldn't..." his voice sounded small and old and sick. Tom's eyes stared back at me, and he shook his head back and forth, back and forth. *No, No, No.* We said nothing to each other. I drove like hell. The only sound inside Betsy was Dad's weak voice weeping out of him.

I'm standing outside the church now.

I look up at the three churches. Their long, sharp shadows slice down across the ground around me like tombstones made of coal marking the spot where the flesh-heads engulfed Mom. I like to think they ate all of her, instead of making her into one of them.

The crows are quiet and still as they stare down at me with bottomless black eyes, clad in winged black suits like strange guests at this funeral in my brain. A brown candy bar wrapper that used to hold a *Snickers* tumbles by. My stomach howls in chorus with the wind.

I know there is no food to be found in town, and I know there are no survivors. That's what the routine used to be about, but not anymore. Now it's just about remembering how things used to be. For a long time, I wanted what happened to Mom to be my fault. Something so terrible has to be someone's fault, right? But it's not anyone's fault. Dad could have done things differently, but he didn't. He couldn't, cause that's just how he was built. He did what he thought was best.

WE TAKE CARE OF OUR OWN.

I pull my bike up, time to head back. Time to go home and remember the last of it like I do every day. I think about getting more chalk, but I know the shelf in the Drug Store where the chalk used to sit in yellow boxes is long empty. That nub of chalk I used this morning is the last piece. I think that's fine, though.

I strap my shotgun across my back, and hop onto my seat; one foot on a pedal while the other paws at the ground twice and I'm moving. I'm not going to listen to my mp3 player, because I want to listen to the quiet country while I ride. Just the wind is fine by me today.

I ride along our fence, the farmhouse's pointed brow rising up in the distance. I turn down the long lane, and drink in the empty landscape with my eyes.

It all lays flat before me like a painting. The farmhouse and its structural siblings; the silos, the stables, and the barn dot the land. The barn swallows swim and swoop on the air between the buildings like a school of fish. The sun has gone from white to yellow, and soon enough will burn orange as it slides down the sky. I feel like I did when I was a kid, out playing all day, and as the day ran away from me, it would pull me home. I can feel a smile creep across my face at the sight of it all. Home.

WE TAKE CARE OF OUR OWN...or at least we try.

I could go inside, but it's not time yet. In the old days, when spring and summer came like cousins, you couldn't keep me inside. Those were the days to be barefoot, to run and ride, to swim and search for trails that led to secret fields and hollows. I think of those days and I'm tired of being inside.

Dad used to always say a porch was a place to sit and think, about what a man had done that day, and what he would do the next.

I sit in the rocker, my rifle lying across my legs. The view is the same as it's always been from this spot; the barn and the stables, and between them, the flat fallow fields over which the setting sun will soon hang. Tom and I used to sit here watching the horizon, always wondering what might rise up tiny from below its far off line. On most days it would be the lone shape of a combine, the yellow deer frozen upon its green shell barely visible. We would wish the combines away, and dream aloud that a lone cowboy might ride up out of the void where the sun and moon pass each other at twilight. But that never happened.

My brother wails beneath the house, as if to say, "*Stop daydreamin' about cowboys that never come little brother...get back to the worst part...the part about how I wound up a flesh-head stuck in this lightless box in the basement...*"

When we got home, we took Dad upstairs, and laid him in his bed. We even put him on his side next to his orange bottle of blood pressure pills, and a picture of him and mom that would be covered in blood soon enough.

Tom sobbed and spit words of comfort to Dad, telling him it was going to be okay. I stood apart from them, unable to stop staring at the huge, horseshoe-shaped bite between Dad's thumb and forefinger. It was not going to be okay. I knew it, and Dad knew it.

Dad had been a mess in the truck, but he was all done being broken up.

"Take a knee, boys..." he said. Tom cried even harder, as if he knew exactly what Dad was going to ask of us. Normally, Dad would have told him to knock it off, but he didn't do that now. He shushed him like Mom used to when we were little. That made me cry for the first time that night.

Dad quieted Tom, then he looked at me. His eyes made me a man right then and there. Dad's eyes asked me to do what he knew Tom wouldn't be able to do, and my eyes promised him I would.

"You need to put me down, Dale. I'd prefer to die now, while I still know who I am," Dad said in a slow, certain voice.

WE TAKE CARE OF OUR OWN...except when we can't.

I knew right then I wouldn't be able to do it either.

Tom and I went out into the hall. I hoped that my big brother would get back to himself. That he would dry his eyes, look down at me, and tell me what we were going to do. He didn't. He shut the door quietly behind him, and leaned against it, rolling around and sliding down its length, folding into a seated ball at the foot of the door. I tried talking to Tom, but he just tilted his head back, knocking it with a slow, dull thud against the door at first. He knocked it back harder and harder, over and over. He was crying again.

I knew when Jimmy Berchgot bit, it was three days of the fever.

It always started with the fever.

Three days, then death came to take your soul, with the zombie maker right behind him, ready to load a fuel-injected flesh-eating engine into you, turning you into one mean zombie machine. *VROOM, VROOM MOTHERFUCKER.*

"Tom, Dad wants us to..." I couldn't say it, and I didn't have to. Tom flew up off the floor, grabbing me by the shirt, and slamming me into the wall.

"I know what Dad wants, and I don't give a shit..." His face untwisted, and his hands released my shirt, falling away from me. I could see his mind searching itself, working it out.

"We've got three days, Tom."

"That was just Jimmy Berch..." Tom said, talking to the air.

"…And Mrs. Patterson, and Bill Cotter's wife…" I said right back.

"…Dad's stronger than all those other people were. Maybe it'll take longer…"

I shot him an angry look. He was supposed to handle this. He was supposed to be braver than me. Tom looked down at the floor, like he used to when he was young and didn't want to do something. He drew in a big breath, and it came back out in a sobbing sound. Then he was still.

"That's Dad in there, Dale," Tom said.

I stared at him as if to say, I know Tom, *but what the fuck do we do now?* "I can't put him down when it's still Dad. I want however many days are left with him, and if he turns…" I looked away. "…when he turns, I'll be the one to do it." I didn't believe him.

Tom went back in to sit with Dad, and I watched him holding Dad's hand from the doorway.

For three days, the fever raged through Dad. When I put my hand on him, it was like touching a furnace. The bitch of it was Dad said he was getting colder and colder, teeth chattering so hard I thought they'd break in his mouth, while that freezing fire roared inside him, burning his human insides black, hollowing them out for the zombie engine that was on its way.

On the third day, the fever was done, and Dad was talking again. Tom sat at the foot of his bed, foolishly happy and grinning a big dumb smile at me. He nodded constantly as if to say, *See little brother…Dad's fine. Dad's going to be okay. Dad's not going to try and eat our faces off…*

I asked Dad how he felt, and he just said, "Cold all over, son." He looked at me again with his asking eyes, and then I saw something else behind them. I saw Dad's life flickering out, the winds of his wasted insides blowing hard, and heard the zombie mechanics rumbling closer in their big red, wrecker of a truck.

I told Tom to go and get Dad some water. He toddled out of the room. I waited until I heard his boots fall on the steps, and then I locked the door.

I moved to my father, but held my rifle at the ready. He looked up at me for the last time as himself, and smiled, closing his eyes, flushing thick streams of tears down his pale face.

"I love you, Da-…" He gasped a long, dull noise that ended with a final, gurgling breath. His hands pulled the sheets up into cloth clumps.

His skin drew tight, and the lines of his face deepened like he had aged a hundred years before my eyes.

I choked on my tears, spitting and mewing, and wanting only to throw myself down onto my Dad, but then I remembered. I stepped back. Slow at first, then more quickly, not looking anywhere but at my dead father's body on his bed. My back met the door, and feeling its real wood against my shoulders was all I needed to come back from the weightless world of my grief. I leveled my shotgun, pumped it slowly...*SHUCK. SHUCK*...and leaned into it, feeling the stock settle into its familiar spot between my arm and shoulder.

Tom's boots flew up the steps, down the hall, and the doorknob turned hard against my backside.

"Dale?" There was a silence, then the doorknob turned left and right, left, right, until it was shuddering up and down; Tom trying to rip the door open from outside in the hall. "GODDAMMIT, DALE! OPEN THE FUCKING DOOR!"

My eyes stayed on Dad's corpse. His face a frozen mask of surprise. His hands still gripping the sheets in sweaty bunches.

His right hand sprung open, leaving the sheets in a twisted tower that did not crumble.

"PLEASE LET ME IN, DALE! LET ME IN!" Tom pounded on the door now with both hands. I felt the wood trembling at my back.

Dad's fingers danced, driven by the pistons of the zombie engine that was rumbling to life inside him. My gaze drifted up to see Dad staring at me with new eyes. They were blank, but they were also filled with a horrible, searching thing that saw me. His mouth open wide now, and Dad howled his new self into the world.

"DAD! DAD IS THAT YOU!?! DAAAAAAAAAAAAAAD!" The door bulged behind me as Tom threw himself against it. It wouldn't be long now. I sniffed hard now, clearing the sad snot out of my nose, and shaking the tears out of my eyes. I leaned firmly against the rifle that my father gave me.

Dad dragged his legs off the bed, and they thud-thumped onto the wood floor. His hips hitched forward pulling the rest of him up. His arms fanned out, steadying himself, then he stepped toward me. My finger crept inside the steel trigger guard.

WE TAKE CARE OF OUR OWN.

I know you probably think you'd be able to do it, but let me tell you something. I doubt it.

The door exploded inward knocking me flat on my face. My shotgun skittered across the floor in front of me.

The room hung sideways from where I sprawled on the floor. Tom stumbled in. He stopped for a moment, but the thing-that-was-once-our Dad did not stop. He kept on trucking toward his oldest boy, faster and faster.

"Dad...Dad, it's going to be okay...it's going to be just fine." Tom threw his arms around him. Dad's dead face hung wooden over Tom's shoulder for a moment, then his eyes switched back and forth as he sniffed at the air. His mouth opened like a steam shovel and his entire face fired into Tom's throat, vanishing for a moment. When Dad's head snapped back, he wore a mask of his son's blood.

Tom's screams pitched higher and higher. I scrambled for my shotgun and up onto my knees. My brother pulled himself away, flailing down onto our parent's bed, and Dad stood there chewing and savoring a mouthful of his oldest boy's throat flesh, enjoying his first and last meal.

I did not miss.

The shotgun blast sheared the top left half of Dad's face and head off. His body kicked back straight into the wall and fell like a broomstick onto the floor. His arm folded at a wrong angle beneath him, and his head hung crooked from his neck. He shrieked one last time. His face was now a grisly two-faced mask. One side a jagged, gapping hole, and the other what was left of Dad. His lone eye stared out at me, then the zombie engine behind it sputtered and hissed to sleep.

Tom lay on the bed, arms and hands windmilling from the gaping bite in his throat to his sides, sweeping wet, red angel wings on the white sheets as if they were snow. With each gargling breath, his blood spurted and streamed down his front in a crimson bib.

It all played like TV without sound as I stood there between my twice-dead father and dying brother. I'd like to say that details I had always failed to remember suddenly got clear in that moment, but it was just the opposite. It felt more like a great, living dark surrounded us, and as it crept in, the three of us stood beneath a great, white spotlight that shone down from above. But the dark kept coming, flowing over Dad and Tom, until it was just me standing alone in a column of hot, white light. My entire world just fell away.

It was a hell of a job getting Tom down into the basement, but I knew that's where he had to go.

I dragged Dad's mattress downstairs first, swabbing a bloody trail down the steps and through the kitchen. I got a stack of magazines from Tom's bedroom. Guns and Ammos, Car and Driver, and I even threw in a Time magazine or two, and one of my Playboys for good measure. I'm not really sure why; I doubted flesh-heads read, but something about it made me feel good.

"Gonna be okay, Tom. Just gettin you all set up, big brother." Tom's head was slumped forward, chin on his chest, and his breath crackled like busted glass. Every ragged breath dispensed a new bloody bib from his torn throat.

Finally, I got one of Dad's work lights that he'd clamp to the hood of his truck so that he could work at night when he wanted to. The light was a green plastic half-shell that cradled a 100-watt light bulb with a long power chord snaking down from its head. I didn't want Tom to have to be alone in the dark, (just alone in the light that would burn out in a month or so). Then he would be alone in the dark and a flesh head.

I put the mattress in the shelter. It fit snug in the corner. Then I clipped the light to one of the exposed pipes and plugged it into the wall. It popped on, throwing a sad, small skirt of raw light down along the dull grey wall.

I stepped back, looking at the bomb shelter, and thought it still looked like a tomb, even with a mattress, a not too shabby stack of magazines, and a reading light.

I grabbed Tom by his armpits, and dragged him inside, laying him softly on the mattress. That's when he started to talk, or try to talk.

"Hey lil' bruvver..." He took deep sucking breaths trying to form words, but just drew more blood up into his mouth, until he was coughing and choking, spitting and spraying blood up into the air that rained back down onto his face.

"I'm sorry Tom. I'm really sorry." I didn't cry at all until after. That seemed unfair to me, considering what I was doing to him.

I used both hands to shut the big metal door. It made the loudest clang I ever heard. I sat down on the wall in the dark and waited, listening to the last of the human sounds my brother would make. His bite had been much worse than Dad's so death and the zombie mechanics were working hand in hand on this one. Tom was quiet in about three hours, and then he rose up anew.

He would moan and scratch and beat on that door every night. After awhile I took to playing Metallica to drown him out. Like I said, it was his favorite band, and I thought that maybe even as a flesh head he'd still like them.

WE TAKE CARE OF OUR OWN.

I knew that I would never be able to put Tom down. What's worse is that, I didn't want to. I thought to myself, so what if my brother's a flesh head. He's still my brother isn't he? I had to keep him. I know how it sounds, like he's some kind of pet and not my brother. He couldn't hurt me in the bomb shelter, and I wouldn't have to hurt him. Sure, it's fucked up, but so is a zombie apocalypse. Like I said, you think you know how you'd act if you were standing in my shoes, but you have no idea.

I look out at the twilight sky. Its blue has darkened to purple, and further down hangs the sun, now fat and orange. Below the purple sky darkening into night, the last bands of the day burn yellow, orange, and pink at the rim of the world. I can't help but smile when the first silhouette staggers small out of the setting sun. It's not a cowboy. No, it's a flesh head.

Feels like the last stand I've been itching for.

Suddenly, there is a great line of them rising up in their shaky lockstep over the horizon, stretching across the edge of everything. It's been a long time since I saw a swarm like this. Maybe it means that they've finally won. Maybe they've eaten everyone on the coasts, and now their sweeping the middle of the country for scraps. Or maybe this is their new cycle, a great wandering migration back and forth that will never stop until something vanquishes them like they vanquished us. Maybe the earth itself will catch the zombie virus and its trees and shrubs will feast on the walking dead. Or maybe I'm just tired. I'm so tired and hungry.

Tom bellows like an idiot below the house, full of noise and furious hunger. I wonder if he can feel his new brothers and sisters coming to bust him out. Or maybe it's just the beginning of his night song like always.

I look back out at the darkening world. The line of flesh heads marches relentlessly across the desolate farmland, bringing the night with them. They'll be here soon enough.

When the dead rose up, no one really knew why. There was talk of government conspiracies. It was a US military project gone wrong. It was

China. It was Iran. Some said it was global warming that did it; mother nature's final revenge. What do I think? I think God wanted to show us what we'd become. We were already zombies if you ask me. Mindless things made more mindless by reality TV, content to live our lives on Facebook, texting and twitting; working, eating, shitting, fucking, and just making a huge goddamned mess of things. God, or the universe, or whatever the fuck, decided to have a laugh and said, "Well, you're ruining and eating everything else, so why not each other..." I know that's a depressing thought, but it's the only one that makes sense to me. We're not in this shit because Barack Obama wanted zombie soldiers. Nope, we did it to ourselves.

I'm standing in the basement. It's cool and dark and quiet, except for my brother's raging behind the steel door of the bomb shelter. It bucks on its tracks.

I start forward and each step reminds me of the best and worst things. Dad telling Tom and I, "Us Nolan's, we take care of our own." I see his empty eyes staring at me from his head hanging crooked after I shot him.

I pull my mp3 player out of my front pocket, and think of when Mom gave it to me. Her smiling face framed by her hair like curled cornsilk. She's pulled screaming beneath a raft of hands.

I've always tried to do the best I could through all this shit, but in the end I guess it wasn't enough. Is it ever?

I am my brother's keeper, and I am going to finally take care of my own.

There's no more food for me, and there won't be. I bet my brother's just as hungry as I am.

I slide the mp3 player into its cradle with a kissing click and roll my finger in a silent circle around its dial, scrolling for songs. I settle on METALLICA, just above MOTLEY CREW.

A bell chimes, once, twice, and then Lar's and James Hetfield's drums and guitars fire like a chorus of cannons. *For Whom The Bell Tolls.* It's my brother's favorite song.

I unlock the door, and pull it rumbling to the side. I step back, looking into the inky black of the doorway. My brother wobbles out of the room's deepest dark, and his dead eyes glint in the gloom. I see the bloody bib, now black and thick, that stains his front in a glistening, crusted sheet. I hear the clicking of his teeth.

WE TAKE CARE OF OUR OWN.

The corners of his mouth have split, as if he's been trying to eat the air night after night, gnashing desperately at the shadows. He wears a permanent joker's grin. Below his dead face, his throat gapes at me with its own misshapen mouth that is Tom's zombie birthmark.

I step forward to meet him in the darkness. I think of those nameless flesh heads who will be flowing through our house eventually, and know this is the only way. I won't let them have me. I will give myself to my brother.

WE TAKE CARE OF OUR OWN.

I just hope he eats all of me, because I don't want to come back like him.

Artists

Samantha Lahue - Samantha is self-taught artist with a penchant for the macabre and a passion for protecting children everywhere from the walking dead. Zombies Beware: She's got a sharpened hairbrush handle! See more art at http://www.flickr.com/people/ICStarzz/ or follow her on Twitter @ICStarzz

Sonya May - An aspiring Olympic Rifle Shooter, an aspiring sound engineer, a black belt, and an excellent baker. In the event of a Zombie Apocalypse my weapons of choice would be between an AR-15 and a Remington 870 pump action shotgun. Sonya can be found on Twitter as @ Chizel852

Natalie Cutrufello - Natalie is an artist currently living in Loveland, CO. She studied illustration at the University of the Arts in Philadelphia and now works primarily as a freelance illustrator. At least when she's not battling the undead hordes. Find Natalie on Twitter under the handle @paintedgrenades and watch out because her weapon of choice is a shovel.

The Zombie Survival Crew™ Leaders

 Juliette Terzieff - Former war correspondent, Juliette is at home on the front lines, used to watching bullets fly and bombs explode. She gave birth to Zombie Survival Crew™ and has been the fearless, or is that fearful, leader from the start. This crossbow twirling dynamo is frequently seen on twitter (@jterzieff) running around in circles, screaming her head off, babbling about one life crisis or another, so one might lean more to the fearful side, but let one report of a walker cross her path and her crossbow becomes a fearsome thing to behold—ask anyone who has been on the wrong side of it during a suspected mutiny of her beloved crew. When it comes to crisis of the global cataclysmic kind, rather than the petty day to day issues, you'll hear the twang of the crossbow and find no better person to lead a successful rout on the enemy.

Website: www.julietteterzieff.com

Facebook: www.facebook.com/JulietteTerzieff

 Norman Reedus - He may be the quiet leader, but faced with the undead and Norman roars into action. The most professionally trained of the crew, he wields his crossbow with precision—and has been known to toss a squirrel or two—as Daryl Dixon of *The Walking Dead*. Lest you assume he is a one-trick pony, think again. Norman can be seen laying waste to scumbags right and left in *The Boondock Saints*, pairing humor with handguns and a whole boatload of badass.

Website: www.bigbaldhead.com

Facebook: www.facebook.com/normanreedus

Jinxie G - Suspected of nightly slayings with keyboard in hand, this romance writer will make you fall in love, then rip your heart out—or let one of her many creations do it for her. Leading an army of vampires, werewolves, demons, and angels, this author has also let loose some zombies—and the question remains, will they fight with us or against us? The Zombie Survival Crew™ is glad to have this compound bow wielding Amazon on our side. Nocturnal by nature, you'll find Jinxie chatting up the Twittersphere as @Jinxie_G, tweeting out movies, and keeping the other nocturnes company, leaving the question in our minds—Is this Zombie Survival Crew™ leader a vampire in disguise?
Website: jinxiesworld.wordpress.com
Facebook: www.facebook.com/jinxieg

Anthony Guajardo - This handsome heartthrob may be young, but he definitely has the chops to be a full-fledged leader of the Zombie Survival Crew™. As one of the Vatos on *The Walking Dead*, he proved his stones by facing down zombies and rednecks alike. Not only good-looking, this guy is smart—he was among the first to figure out that the Unnamed Government Agency (UGA) may not be the allies they proclaimed—and brave—leading the rescue attempt for our fearless leader, Juliette. A lover of animals, Anthony is currently putting together a lethal four-legged army to assist in the attack during the Zombiepocalypse. In fact, our biggest concern is not whether he can handle dispatching a horde of zombies, but whether he will survive the crush of girls who will mob him as his star status rises—because he won't be able to use his machete on his fans. Anthony hangs out on twitter as @AnthonyGuajardo—stop by, follow him, and say hi.
Facebook: www.facebook.com/Anthony.Guarajdo

R.C. Murphy - The best *secret weapon* the Zombie Survival Crew™ has. When the undead start walking, they'll have to make it through the hailstorm of one-liners this funny woman hurls—they'll start splitting their sides which means a slower approach and more time for us to get to battle stations and muster the brigades. For a taste of her humor, check her out on twitter—@RCMurphy. She spends most of her time hiding out in her cave, and is easily spooked, but lest we forget, she doesn't only slay with her wit, she twirls a mean sword and tarries with the vampires she writes, and those who get close enough will soon be missing their head.

Website: rcmurphy.wordpress.com

Facebook: www.facebook.com/RC.Murphy.Writer

Robert "IronE" Singleton - One piercing laser glare from those eyes, and the zombies will turn tail and run the other way. As T-Dog on *The Walking Dead*, IronE shows his strength and ability to fight the undead, but underneath the tough exterior is a big, huggable teddy-bear. We're happy he throws his hammer down for our team, because none of us would want to face him in battle. Give him a shout out on twitter (@IronESingleton) and if he's not busy out slaying zombies or working on another production, he'll give you a shout back.

Website: www.ironesingleton.com

Facebook: www.facebook.com/pages/IronE-Singleton/116408841720422

LK Gardner-Griffie - Definitely the dark horse of the Crew, questions abound as to whether this leader is a mole from the UGA. Either way, the Zombie Survival Crew™ feels the best course of action is to keep this one close. Her disguise as an award winning writer of Middle Grade/Young Adult fiction may be the best we've ever seen. The most anyone can get out of her on the topic of why she's a member of the Zombie Survival Crew™ is that she hates zombies and the only good zombie is one who is made dead permanently. LK's plan in the event of a

Zombiepocalypse is to hop in her flux capacitor and go back far enough in time to set the crew in motion. And this is why she has been dubbed the Oracle—for always being one step ahead. *We really hope she's on our side.* Follow her on twitter (@lkgg) and see if you can help us pierce through the sunny, supportive camouflage to discover the mystery beneath the facade.

Website: www.griffieworld.com

Facebook: www.facebook.com/AuthorLKGardnerGriffie

Neil Brown, Jr. - For charm and sweetness, you need look no further than our First Lieutenant Extraordinaire. But make no mistake, when the undead rise and start shambling your way, Neil's katana will be unsheathed and zombies will fall left and right. We came to know Neil as the wise-crackin' Guillermo on *The Walking Dead*, but he has proven his metal in support of the crew. Make sure you stop by and say hello to Neil on Twitter as @1neilbrownjr,

Website: www.neilbrownjr.com

Facebook: www.facebook.com/Neilbrownjr